TWO STRAIGHTS TOO MANY

ROMEO ALEXANDER

ROMEO ALEXANDER

Editing by Jo Bird
Beta Reading by Melissa R

ELIAS

*L*ightning flashed against the coal-black sky, illuminating the rain-drenched street. Elias instinctively ticked down the seconds before the crash of thunder followed it. His mother had always told him that every second between lightning and thunder meant a mile between him and the impact. He wasn't sure if it was true or not, but he'd been in the habit of counting for well over twenty years.

That bolt had struck five miles away.

Gripping the wheel tighter, Davis leaned forward to squint out the front of the truck's huge windshield.

"Oof, this storm don't look like it's letting up anytime soon," Davis muttered.

Elias shrugged. "Makes our job easier."

"I still say it would have gone out without us," Davis added.

Elias only shrugged again, not willing to argue over it. The fire had, thankfully, been easily put out. The storm had been waning and waxing for the past day and had drenched the entire city. Fortunately, that meant they'd only needed to contend with the pizzeria, rather than also worrying about the fire spreading to the nearby stores and restaurants that made up the business district of Port Dale.

That didn't mean it would have gone out on its own. It had engulfed the small building by the time Elias and the rest of their team had shown up. And even if the buildings surrounding it were soaked and resistant to the flames, Elias knew it wouldn't have necessarily stayed that way.

Davis glanced over at him. "You're quieter than usual."

Elias grunted. "Pay attention to the road. Last thing we need is to crash into someone and make today even longer."

He had so been hoping his double shift wouldn't lead to any trouble. He should have known better. Just as he was about to hit the twenty-four-hour mark, the station alarm had gone off, and he'd been thrown into action. By the time they got back and worked their way through the entire report and cleanup procedure, he would have been on shift for nearly thirty-six hours. The call of his bed was a siren's song, and his sore, dirty body ached to crawl between the sheets and pass out for as long as he could.

"I'm not going to crash," Davis protested.

"You will if you keep worrying about me instead of the road."

"Grumpy ass."

"I'm tired man, let me be."

Davis grunted but didn't follow-up. Everyone in the station had had their fair share of long shifts in the past, and everyone dealt with it differently. Some of them, Davis being one of them, became downright foul when they hit a certain threshold of tiredness. Elias typically just wanted to be left alone. But the obscuring rain was making him more tense than the fight with the pizzeria fire had. All he wanted was to get back to the station in one piece so he could trudge through the rest of his shift.

Davis had come good on his promise, though, and got them back without incident. Gunning the fire truck into the station, Davis stopped just short of the thick, bright yellow line painted on the floor to signify the parking space. Elias ignored Davis' wicked grin, knowing full well the man was just being smug because he was the most skilled at handling the truck while Elias was, at best, passable. It was a source of humor for the rest of the crew. Elias was the tallest and broadest of the men at the station, and should theoretically have practice navigating something big into small spaces.

Davis chuckled as they hopped out of the truck, going around the front to meet Elias. "Why don't you go get cleaned up?"

Elias glanced at the truck, frowning. "Cleanup first."

"I think I can manage it, I actually got some sleep before I came in. Just go soak in the showers for half an hour, then we can get the report out of the way."

It was tempting. Enough so that Elias wasn't going to pass up the opportunity. It didn't matter how small a fire was, fighting them always left him feeling drained. Coupled with his sleep deprivation, Elias wondered if he would even make it out of the shower before collapsing on the floor and napping under the warm spray instead.

"Alright, just don't break anything," Elias muttered as he walked off.

With a hefty yawn, Elias trudged through the garage and into the living quarters of the station. As he walked the length of the hallway, he listened to the sounds of a muffled conversation coming from the chief's office. Recognizing the man's tone as all business, Elias figured he'd have at least that half-hour promised by Davis before he had to deal with the chief. The next door on his right led to the kitchen area, where the scent of what smelled like chili wafted out. Elias glanced in, spotting Keith by the stove, humming to himself merrily as he stirred the steaming pot in front of him. Elias raised a hand in greeting as their eyes met but continued on his way.

At the end of the hall were a set of doors, one on each side. To the right was the common area, where the men on shift could relax and laze about as they played games or watched TV. Or if they wanted, they could go through the door at the back of the room and collapse on one of the bunkbeds set along the walls.

Elias, however, swerved toward the left-hand door, which opened up into the small locker room. Rubbing his face, he stumbled to his locker and popped it open. Undressing, he threw his dirty clothes into the bin for whoever was on laundry duty to take care of. He caught movement out of the corner of his eye and glanced over, wincing when he realized it had been his own reflection in the full-length mirror on the wall.

His face was still smeared with soot and dirt, and somehow it had managed to get onto his arms, legs, and hands as well. His normally bronzed skin, inherited from his father, shone from the residual sweat of being stuffed into layers of protective clothing and battling a fire. Leaning toward the mirror, he pulled at the lower lids of his eyes, looking at the red rims below the blue irises and massaged the dark circles beneath them. He looked like hell, but thankfully it was nothing a good wash and a long rest wouldn't solve.

Grunting, he snatched up his toiletry bag and closed his locker. Padding through the open doorway, he entered the shower room. Privacy wasn't exactly a demand in the firehouse, and whoever had designed the shower room had apparently known that. There were no individual stalls, just lines of showerheads along three walls, and a drain in the middle. Not that Elias cared, his high school days of football in the autumn, wrestling in the winter, and baseball in the spring had left him not only with frequent exposure to the naked male body but exposing his own as well.

A groan escaped him as he stepped beneath a rush of warm water from one of the showerheads. It wasn't as good as sleeping, but it was a solid second-place prize in his opinion. The tension in his broad shoulders eased as the water beat down on him, pattering onto the tiled floor. Silently, Elias thanked whoever had designed the showers and made sure the water pressure was high enough to beat the living hell out of sore muscles.

"Bad one?"

The sudden presence of a voice made Elias jump, and he winced as he smacked his head against one of the showerheads. The place must have been designed for people six feet and under because the showerheads always posed a threat to him. Wincing, he rubbed his head, then wiped the water out of his face as he turned to see who the hell had snuck up on him.

Elias grunted. "Evening, Matt. I really wish you'd let us put a bell on you."

The sandy-haired man grinned. "Sorry big guy, wasn't trying to scare you."

"No, you're just really good at it."

"It's a gift."

Elias watched as Matt made his way to his own showerhead, several feet away from Elias. It wasn't often that Matt would bathe with the others in the station. Not because of any modesty on his part, Matt simply had the honor of being the only gay man to work at station 231. There were a few of the men who weren't totally comfortable with it, though most of them at least had the decency to keep it to themselves. Matt wasn't stupid, though, and generally tried to save himself and others the trouble and chose to bathe alone, or only when certain people were around.

Elias just happened to be one of those people. His best friend, Cade, liked to tease Elias that Matt had a thing for seeing Elias naked. Apparently, Matt's boyfriend, whose name Elias had yet to learn, resembled Elias on a superficial level. The thing was, Elias really didn't give a shit if Matt was gay or if he happened to like looking at his naked body. He also suspected that Matt's comfort with him had more to do with the lack of fucks Elias gave than with any physical attraction.

"Where's your boyfriend?" Matt asked, a smirk on his face.

Elias rolled his eyes, turning back to his shower. The fire-fighters of Station 231 thought it was the absolute pinnacle of wit to refer to Elias and Cade as boyfriends. Everyone was well aware that they were both straight, especially with Cade's womanizing habits. Yet, because the two of them were close, everyone, Matt included, took turns making jokes.

"Where's *yours*?" Elias asked.

"Eh, out of town. Visiting his mom for her birthday."

"Nice of him."

"She's all he's got, well, and his sister. They're pretty close."

Once upon a time, he might have said the same thing about his own family. After his father died from an accident when Elias had been ten, his mother and three siblings had grown even closer. He supposed they were still close and that distance, even if that distance involved being on the other side of the country, didn't really change that. Still, being so far away meant it was all too easy to get caught up in his life and forget to call. His mother, thankfully, was far more diligent than he was and called him at least once a week.

"But seriously, where is Cade? Don't you two normally work the same shift?" Matt asked.

They did, though that wasn't necessarily because of any choice by Elias or Cade. The Chief had decided at some point that the two of them were better working together than they were separately. Elias had a sneaking suspicion that was because the chief honestly believed Elias might have a restraining effect on Cade. His best friend was as energetic and outgoing as Elias was reserved and measured. Elias had yet to have any real success getting Cade to do anything, however. He was content to allow the whirlwind that was his friend to blow through an area and watch the chaos.

"He's at home as far as I know," Elias told him.

Okay, he happened to know for a fact that Cade was crashed on his couch, binge-watching some show on Netflix. Cade had been texting him throughout the entire day with a long line of commentary about the show. Elias still had no idea what the show was about, as the majority of Cade's comments had been about random things the characters had said, the bad CGI effects, and a few comments about something stupid someone was wearing. When it came to Cade, you were bound to get a lot of information, but that didn't guarantee it would be helpful information.

"He'll be in tomorrow," Elias continued.

"Please tell me he didn't call in 'sick' today," Matt laughed.

Elias snorted. "No, he knows damn well the Chief knows the difference between him being sick, and him having the tequila flu."

Matt ran his hands through his hair. "You have tomorrow off?"

"Naw, I still have a few days before all that. I do get to go home and play dead for several hours before I have to worry about it, though," Elias said with relish.

"How long you been on?"

"Almost thirty-six now."

"Ugh."

"Tell me about it. I feel like I'm dead but somehow still walking around."

Matt snorted, twisting off the water. "Well, get yourself home. We don't need you passing out around here. Not sure we have enough guys on the clock at the moment to move your dead weight."

"I'll do my best," Elias said with a roll of his eyes.

Matt stalked off after that, and even with the floor flooded with water, managed not to make a sound as he left. Elias always thought the man had missed his calling as a private detective considering how stealthy he was.

He'd just managed to resume enjoying his shower when Davis' voice rang out. "Nice to see you didn't die."

Elias sighed, hanging his head. "I'm not going to get a peaceful shower today, am I?"

"I'd be more worried about Cade finding out you were in here with Matt," Davis said.

Elias turned around, looking into the locker room with a frown. He didn't see Matt, but that didn't mean the guy wasn't still within earshot. Davis had a notoriously big mouth, and he was even more known for not thinking before he spoke.

"Don't be an ass, Davis. I know it's hard for you, but just try," Elias told him.

Davis held up his hands. "Damn, it was just a joke."

It was more than a joke, and they both damn well knew it too. Davis, right along with another firefighter in the station, Keith, outright refused to undress, let alone shower, when Matt was around. Personally, Elias thought it was the stupidest thing he'd ever heard.

"I'm not dating Cade, and quit being a dick about Matt," Elias growled.

"I'm not being a dick."

"I'm tired, not stupid and blind, Davis."

It wasn't like either Davis or Keith were subtle about not wanting to be naked around Matt. Out of the two, though, Elias would begrudgingly admit that Davis was the better behaved. Keith always seemed a hair's breadth away from a nasty comment when he was around Matt. And Elias had seen Keith's expression when Matt's boyfriend had dropped him off at the station once, and given him a goodbye peck. Keith had looked like someone had force-fed him hot sewage.

"Right, well, if you're done being the champion of the people, the Chief wants us," Davis said, jabbing a thumb over his shoulder.

"Ugh, I was hoping he'd be on his call for a while longer," Elias sighed.

"No such luck. He wants to see us. Told him you needed to crash, though, so maybe he'll go easy on us," Davis told him.

Elias turned off his shower and padded out to where he'd left his towel. "Thanks for taking care of the cleanup."

"Eh, you look like you're about ready to drop. You deserved to soak a bit."

Elias nodded wearily, wrapping the towel around his waist. Maybe if he didn't sleep the entire night and morning away, he might wake up and soak in his tub before the next shift. God knows he'd had a large tub installed in his apartment for a reason, he might as well get as much use out of it as he possibly could.

"Alright, let's get this over with," Elias groaned.

CADE

*R*eaching into his pocket, Cade slid out his phone to check the time. Sighing, he pushed it back into the safety of his pants. Leave it to his mother to make him wait. Now, if the shoe were on the other foot, he could have expected half a dozen calls from her the moment she didn't see him at the precise time they agreed to meet. She, however, was nearly twenty minutes late and hadn't sent one message.

"Typical," he grumbled, shifting impatiently from one foot and to the other.

He glanced over his shoulder, forcing a smile as a woman came strolling out of the cafe he was standing outside. The place was far more upscale than he would have chosen, but his mother had insisted. There was a small seating area dotted with little tables, perfect for intimate conversations between two people. Well, he assumed that was the intention anyway. The small area was cordoned off from the busy side-walk by a waist-high metal fence. It wasn't exactly all that secluded, but he supposed it was the thought that counted.

His eyes drifted back toward the woman as she paused

before stepping out onto the sidewalk, rummaging through her purse. While he wasn't quite sure what the point of wearing leggings as pants was, he wasn't going to argue with the results either. Cade was an absolute sucker for a good pair of legs, and sliding them into a pair of tight leggings was one of the quickest ways to get his attention. It was tempting to approach the woman. The whimsical print of frolicking cats with neon colors splashed against the background would have made a perfect excuse to strike up a conversation, as well as subtly covering up the fact that he'd been checking her out.

Instead, he rummaged through his other pocket and pulled out a mangled pack of cigarettes. Stepping away from the cafe and the main street sidewalk, Cade walked a·few feet away. The side street was far less busy than the one in front of the cafe. Making sure to keep his distance from the few people walking by, he pulled a lighter from his pocket and flicked it to life. Sucking deeply, he watched the tip of the cigarette flare to life and felt the bite of the smoke hit the back of his throat.

Sure, his mother would bitch endlessly that he smelled like an ashtray. Technically, he was supposed to have quit and would have been happy to let her continue believing that. He'd forgone a cigarette before showing up, thinking she'd be on time, and not wanting to smell like smoke. Considering she didn't have the decency to even send an apology text with an explanation, however, Cade thought she could suffer through a bit of ashy smell.

A wry voice from his right piped up. "Those will kill you, you know."

Cade blinked, turning to look at the woman who had apparently walked out from the small alley behind the cafe. She was dressed in the black slacks and white button-up he'd seen the employees of the cafe wearing. Her hair was a sheet of shining black, which she tossed over her shoulders with a wicked grin that gripped his attention as surely as the devilish glint in her eyes.

He watched her raise her own cigarette to her lips and grinned. "We're all dying, right?"

"Picking your poison, huh?" she asked.

Glancing at the swell of her breasts against her shirt, he chuckled. "Well, one of them."

If she'd noticed his glance, she didn't seem bothered by it. In fact, the amused tilt to her lips grew stronger. "I'm Julie."

"Cade."

She nodded. "Oh, I know all about you, Cade Masters."

He blinked. "Uh, well, usually when people know my name before I know theirs, I'm either in for a good time or a bad one."

Julie laughed. "I'm May's friend."

That did not help in the slightest. Considering the name didn't immediately click, Cade couldn't only assume it was one of the girls he'd picked up from a bar or club. Those weren't exactly people he filed away in his long term memory.

"You don't remember her, do you?" she asked

"That depends."

"On?"

"Whether or not I'm getting smacked if I answer honestly."

Julie tossed her hair over her shoulder once again, chuckling. "You're safe."

"Right, yeah, don't remember her, sorry."

She shrugged. "Well, I guess that's not a surprise. Someone like you probably doesn't keep a catalog of the girls you've been with."

Cade's brow shot up. "Someone like me?"

She cocked her hip, rolling her eyes. "Yes. A good looking guy who absolutely reeks of womanizer."

Cade frowned, and not just because he hated that term. She was obviously in good spirits, but it was a little difficult to focus on defending himself when Julie was angling her hips toward him. Even with the loose slacks, it wasn't hard to see that she'd been blessed with a good ass as well.

"You make it sound so...dirty," Cade finally protested.

Julie laughed. "Fine, would you prefer I call you a slut?"

Cade winked, pointing at her. "Now, that's a term I can get behind."

"And here I thought your whole goal was to get behind someone, not something."

"I can do both, I'm a man of many talents."

Julie's dark gaze swept over him in obvious appraisement. "So I've been told."

Cade hissed in a breath, wincing. "Ooh, so your friend remembers me."

"Yes, and you don't remember her."

"I feel like this conversation is going to bite me in the ass at some point."

She leaned to the side, looking over his ass. "It's a good one to bite."

Cade drew another cigarette out, lighting it with a grin. "Am I being hit on right now, or are you setting me up just to knock me down?"

"Just how many girls have you pissed off, mister?" she asked, her tone growing even more amused.

"A...few, here and there," he answered honestly.

Which he personally thought was bullshit. It wasn't as though he'd ever lied to any of them. It's why he hated being called a womanizer, it conjured up an image of some greasy sleazeball who would lie and seduce their way into a woman's pants. He never said anything to them that promised any more than one night with him, and the insistence that he would do his absolute best to make sure they had a good time.

"Hmm," Julie hummed thoughtfully. "Weird. May said you were a perfect gentleman."

"Well, I'm glad she enjoyed herself," Cade said, meaning it.

The devilish glint returned to her eyes. "And that you fuck like a champ."

Cade flashed a none too modest grin. "Well, now I'm definitely glad she enjoyed herself."

"I know right, free advertisement."

Cade looked her over, wondering how defined her curves were when out of the loose-fitting outfit. "Question is, is the advertisement finding me another customer?"

"Only if you let me buy you a drink first."

Cade's brow raised. "Oh? Asserting yourself so soon?"

"Oh, you have no idea."

Okay, she'd already had his interest, but now she had his attention.

"Well, with that promise hanging over us, why don't I give you my number, and you can tell me when and where to meet you," Cade offered.

"You don't want mine?" she asked curiously.

Cade shrugged. "If you have mine, you can make it happen whenever. But I know most women aren't too comfortable with guys having their numbers."

She laughed. "Well, I've had a few persistent guys in the past. Then again, I've known a few women who are just as bad. You're telling me your charming ass hasn't had any problems?"

Cade chuckled, rubbing his forearm. "Nothing worth noting."

Julie pulled out her phone. "Alright, give me the number then."

Cade did so, still grinning. "Just give me a shout when you're ready."

Her mouth opened, but her brow furrowed deep. Before Cade could do anything more than wonder what was suddenly wrong, a hand appeared reaching from behind him. A set of perfectly manicured fingers, nails painted a dainty pink, shoved into his vision and clamped down over the cigarette between his lips. Startled, he jerked back as the cigarette was yanked away and tossed to the ground.

"Kaidan Anthony Masters, you told me you had *quit*," his mother's sharp voice rebuked.

Oh hell.

"Hello, mother, it's nice of you to finally show up," Cade said in a tired voice.

Turning his gaze away from the far more preferable sight of Julie, he faced his mother. As per usual, she was dressed smartly, her pantsuit a bold purple, and the customary string of pearls at her neck. Cade didn't think he'd ever seen his mother look anything but ready to meet a very important person at any given moment. Even in his childhood, she was awake well before he was, dressed perfectly, hair perfectly shaped, make-up perfect, and ready to take on the world.

Pamela Masters eyed her son with the hazel eyes she'd passed down to him. "Well?"

Cade turned, shooting Julie an apologetic look. "Talk to you later?"

With her brow still raised, Julie ground her cigarette out. "Yeah, sure. Uh, good luck."

He watched her go, knowing his chances of hearing from her after this mortifying, yet typical display had probably crashed to the dirt. Nothing was sexier than watching a guy get his balls cut off by his mother.

Cade turned back to his mother. "Am I going to get to

hear why you decided to show up almost a half-hour after we were supposed to meet?"

Pamela's thin brow arched sharply. "Do not try to change the subject, Kaidan."

"So that's a no then," he said.

She sniffed daintily. "I was caught up with an important phone call. You know full well that my day is occupied most of the time."

Mm, didn't he know it, and if he ever thought about forgetting, she'd be quick to remind him.

"And which cocktail party are you arranging this time?" he asked in a sugary sweet voice.

She wasn't fooled. "Don't get smart, Kaidan. I would hope by now, you would understand how absolutely important it is that your father and I are both seen and known. Networking is just as important to business as making deals and sales."

Yes, because it had nothing at all to do with his mother's almost pathologic need to be seen, heard, and most importantly, obeyed. His father might have his hands on the wheel when it came to the business, but his mother was the one who held the reins tightly in every other way. Her word was law in the home, and she was the undisputed mistress of all parties, galas, and whatever else she decided to involve herself in.

"What, and I don't get an invite?" Cade asked with mock hurt in his voice.

Pamela's nostrils flared slightly. "The last time you even deigned to be seen at one of my functions, you made a complete fool of yourself and our family."

Cade's lip twitched. "Oh, it wasn't *that* bad."

"You and your...friend, ruined the garden party."

"It was one little section of fencing. How were we

supposed to know you didn't have the thing secured properly?"

"By sitting in a chair like any normal person. And it was more than just the fencing, and you know it."

Cade was trying extremely hard to keep his features as schooled as possible. It was growing difficult, however, as his mother's barely restrained indignation showed through. Poor Elias, the man was honestly just too big for his own good. He'd not so much tried to sit on the fencing, but lean against it for a bit of rest having been dragged to the party by Cade. Elias had been exhausted from a long shift at the station, and his reflexes weren't quite as sharp as they usually were. The poorly secured section of decorative fencing had tumbled backward from Elias' weight and taken him along with it. That alone would have been enough, but there also happened to be a small table next to Elias, and his foot had smacked into it. The delicate statuettes and little vase with crystal flowers in it had gone flying, the sharp sound of shattering glass and hollow clatter of the table hitting the ground had drawn the eyes of everyone at the party.

"Elias was incredibly sorry, and it was an accident," he reminded her.

She sniffed. "He wouldn't have to be sorry if he had been more careful. Honestly, Kaidan, I wish…"

Cade cut her off. "Let's not finish that sentence, Mother."

"I'm allowed to wish good things for my son."

"Not at the expense of my friends, and especially not Elias."

The false cheer in his voice was gone, replaced by what he hoped was a hard enough warning. He was *not* having a discussion about Elias with her. There were plenty of things about his life that she could and did take issue with, and he was resigned to having to listen to her grievances every time they saw one another. It had been a fact of life for his twenty-seven years of living, but even he had his limits.

Her jaw set stubbornly. "I'm sure he's a perfectly nice person, but…"

"How would you know when you won't have anything to do with him?"

"I have had a conversation with him, Kaidan."

"Yes, and you showed him the same courtesy you'd show a dirty stray that wandered up to you."

"Oh, don't be so melodramatic, Kaidan. I was perfectly polite and friendly. You act as if I'm incapable of speaking to someone…"

She trailed off, and he raised a brow. "What, someone poor? Someone not of your station?"

"It's your station as well," she reminded him for the millionth time.

"No, my station is about a mile that way," he said, pointing.

"Honestly, you're going to be twenty-eight years old this year. I think that's quite long enough for you to have grown out of this stage of yours."

He rolled his eyes, glad that she was choosing something else to harp on about. His mother would never admit that she was changing the topic, no, can't admit she might be compromising. And he knew she wasn't compromising out of some sense of respect, but because the last time she'd pushed too hard about Elias, there had been a little bit of a scene. Cade might not like to make an ass out of himself in public, but as she'd learned, he wasn't above drawing attention with a raised voice because of her none too subtle dislike of Elias.

"I don't think anyone goes through the training, sticks around for years as a firefighter, and then somehow outgrows it, Mother. I'm going to go out on a limb and say that I'm probably going to be sticking with it," he told her.

It was the answer she should have been used to hearing, while also being the one she liked the least. Cade had started keeping a mental checklist every time he met with her. While the order of subjects she liked to 'discuss' might be different each time, he almost always left a meeting with her with every mental box checked off.

"And the women?" she asked.

Ah, there's the next box, check.

"I just haven't found the right woman, Mother," he assured her.

"Yes, and if you're anything like I've heard, you're very...diligently making sure to check each and every one over," she said as she turned to walk toward the cafe.

Free of her gaze, Cade grinned. "I like to be thorough."

"Well, honestly, you would do well to comport yourself a little better. Christine still has her eyes on you, and that would be a perfect match," his mother said fondly.

Cade wrinkled his nose. "Yeah, I know you think it would be."

"It would."

Christine Hoffman was on the city council, and on excellent, though thankfully not too friendly terms with his mother. That she also happened to be the one who oversaw most of the public works, including the firefighting stations, was a thorn in Cade's side. Christine was a good looking woman and was undoubtedly a capable one. The problem was, she was way too much like the men and women Pamela was so fond of, which was the opposite of what Cade enjoyed. She was the personification of class and money, which always left a sour taste on Cade's tongue.

And worst of all, she was as persistent, if not more, than his mother was.

"She's a lovely woman and highly intelligent. I think you both would make a lovely pair," Pamela continued, not bothering to see if Cade was even listening.

"I'm sure," Cade said, wondering if his mother was picturing the grandkids yet.

"And as a council member? That would be lovely, imagine," she continued.

Cade rolled his eyes, yes, can't forget that he'd yet to bring anything of note to the family. Better that he marry someone who could do that for him since he was so hellbent on living his own life and career and not the one his parents had wished for him.

"I take it you spoke to her recently," Cade said.

"I did. She attended one of the charity dinners Michael Turner was hosting last weekend."

Sensing his opportunity, Cade feigned interest. "Really? What was the charity?"

"Oh, funding for the homeless shelters around the city, and a few clinics as well. You know how Michael is. He loves to dip his fingers into the pies of the downtrodden," Pamela said, waving a hand.

But despite the dismissive gesture, she continued the story of the dinner. Despite how maddening it was to have an actual conversation with his mother, she always hogged the whole damn thing, it was remarkably easy to get her talking. All he needed to do was make the occasional interested noise, or ask a brief question to show he was at least pretending to care, and she would talk endlessly.

It was a shame the cafe didn't serve harder drinks.

ELIAS

*H*e wasn't sure how long he'd been sleeping, but the bleary edges to his thoughts told him he'd been out for at least an hour. The day before, despite hoping he'd get a lot of sleep, he'd found himself waking up constantly. So once more, he'd dragged himself into the station, barely awake. Even Cade had commented on how tired he looked, which was saying something since he usually looked tired anyway. After the shift had ended, he'd dragged himself back to his apartment to have a nap.

Elias grunted into the couch pillow, not sure if he wanted to be awake yet or not. At the edge of his thoughts, he realized he'd woken up for a reason. However, he couldn't quite remember anything in particular, waking him up. Opening his eyes to stare at the back of the couch, he listened to the quiet of his apartment. After several seconds passed, he heard the soft sound of sliding paper somewhere behind him.

Elias groaned. "Remind me why I gave you a key to my apartment?"

Cade snickered. "Because you love the idea of me sneaking in here to watch you sleep."

"Creep."

"Aw, but you look so cute when you're napping."

"Nothing about me is cute."

"Oh, you look like a hibernating bear."

"Don't you do it."

"What? You don't want me to call you, Osito?"

Elias groaned at the nickname his mother had coined for him years before, and that had followed him around ever since. 'Little bear' had been cute when he'd been a scrawny eight-year-old, and maybe amusing when he'd hit his teens and shot up so high his mother's head barely reached his chest. It had even grown partially fitting when he'd begun to bulk out to his current size, and his body hair had become dark and thick. Yet, even as an adult, he didn't mind his mother's somewhat ironic but ultimately affectionate term for him. She was his mom after all, and like hell was he going to stop her, or try.

Elias rolled over to glare at his best friend. "I hate you."

Cade was sprawled in the massive chair, one long leg thrown over the arm, with his back pressed against the other. A thick book was in one of his hands, propped open on his lap. As much as Cade hated being called a pretty boy, even Elias had to admit the man could pull off being a model if he wanted. He mostly resembled his father, bearing a strong jaw and defined cheekbones, giving him a masculine appearance, yet not so hard as to be blocky. His auburn hair always managed to somehow fall just right, looking casually and carelessly messy no matter what. It was his eyes that drew women's attention more than anything. They were the sole thing Cade had physically inherited from his mother. Thankfully, Cade's bright hazel eyes were typically full of laughter and wry humor rather than the sharp, critical appraisal that Pamela Masters always had.

"What?" Cade asked after the silence stretched.

"Your Spanish is atrocious," Elias told him.

"Your mom always tells me it's good."

"I swear to God, Cade, this better not lead up to some mom sex joke."

Cade looked up, frowning. "We both know your mom is off-limits with jokes. She's a nice lady, I'm not gonna be a dick about her."

Elias grunted. "Right, sorry."

Cade's frown disappeared instantly, giving way to a smirk. "As if I'm going to take offense. We both know you're a grump when you first wake up."

"Especially when I wake up to find an intruder in my chair," Elias said as he pushed himself up.

"Is it really intruding? You gave me the key. That's pretty much an open invitation."

"No, it's not."

"It was for me."

Elias grunted but wasn't going to argue. Cade had far too much practice arguing and even more at twisting words and conversations around to get what he wanted. Growing up with the bulldozer of a mother he had, Cade had honed his skills of misdirection and careful manipulation.

Well, and there was also the fact that Cade was right too. For anyone else but his family and Cade, a key from Elias would have been meant as an emergency thing or given out of necessity. In truth, the two of them spent as much time at one another's place as they did their own apartments. Though if he thought about it, Cade tended to show up at Elias' place more than the reverse.

Elias gave him a sleepy smile. "How's your mom?"

Cade looked up, curling his lip. "Really?"

"Really."

"We both know damn well it was an hour of absolute hell."

"I'd think you'd be immune to her needles and knives."

Cade shrugged, turning his attention back to his book. "I'm over her poking and prodding. It's the boredom of having to pretend like I give a shit that kills me. I'm telling you, hell isn't agony and pain, it's listening to my mother go on and on about charity dinners and the gossip doing the rounds of her social circle. Seriously, why she wants me to marry some high society woman when most of them seem to be cheating on their husbands is beyond me."

"Maybe she just thinks that's to be expected," Elias said.

"Which provides the horrifying idea that she might be doing the same."

"I mean…"

"No, I can't imagine my mother doing anything like that. The woman wouldn't know passion if it bit her on the ass."

"I mean, she had you."

Cade snorted. "And she's never let me live it down since."

Elias remained quiet, unsure what to say as always when Cade's mother and their relationship came up. Elias and his own mother had not always seen eye to eye on things. But there had always been a great sense of warmth and love between the two of them. Between Cade and his mother, however, there was an ocean of animosity and disapproval on both sides. Pamela's attitude toward her son had always struck Elias as one of businesswoman and employee. That Cade didn't fit into her world, into her expectations, brought her the same sort of frustration he imagined someone would have if their own arm started doing what it wanted instead of what was commanded.

"Did get a girl to take my number, though. Whether or

not she'll actually call after seeing my mother in action is a different story," Cade continued.

Elias winced. "Front row seat?"

"Yeah, maybe I should take her to a cage fight if she calls me. It'd be about the same experience."

"Do you actually remember this one's name?"

Cade stuck his tongue out. "Julie. Apparently, one of her friends had uh, already known me."

Elias snorted, rubbing at his sleep-filled eyes. "So all that talk about showing someone a good time wasn't bullshit then."

"I know, right?"

It was a strange facet of their friendship that the conversation didn't bother Elias. Even as a teenager, he'd never been comfortable hearing about his friends' conquests, or hearing anything that placed them into a sexual context. Learning that any of his friends was a good fuck would have been Elias' cue to change the subject. Yet, like with so many things, Cade was an exception.

Even their first meeting had been an exception. Elias was not a man who warmed to people quickly, and people usually didn't take to him too quickly, either. He was a big man, with a serious face, and combined with his reserved manner, it made him come across as big and scary. Yet on Elias' first shift at the station, Cade had been the one to initially look at him and genuinely smile.

And make a joke, of course.

Cade looked up, cocking his head. "What are you smirking about?"

"I'm remembering the first thing you ever said to me," Elias said.

Cade laughed. "Something like 'Jesus fuck, you're a big ass motherfucker. At least now we have someone around here who can reach the top shelf,' wasn't it?"

There had been a playful wink added at the end of the statement, and Cade had taken his hand for a warm handshake. Considering how polite and rigid everyone else's greeting had been, Cade's had been a surprise. Elias had found himself shocked into silence, shaking the hand of the man who was grinning like an idiot. And it had been Cade who had dragged him around the station, showing him everything and teaching him the ins and outs of working there.

Elias still wasn't entirely sure what it was about that tour that had done it, but somewhere along the way, he'd realized he'd made a new friend. He'd never said it aloud, but he had walked away from that shift feeling as though something inside him had slid into place with a quiet click. He didn't know if it had been the same for Cade, but the two of them had become friends rapidly after that, growing more and more close over the past two years.

Cade snorted, shaking his head. "Quit thinking so damn hard. You just woke up, dude."

"Going back to sleep sounds good," Elias admitted.

Cade gave him a knowing smile. "Maybe you should eat first?"

"Yes, Mom."

"Hey, don't make me call your mom."

Elias scowled. "That's cheating."

"Then eat some damn food, and I'll let you sleep the evening away."

Elias let out a wide yawn, stretching his arms out until he felt the stiff muscles pull. "Thanks, Mom. So good I have you to watch out for me."

At a glance, an outside observer who knew about their upbringing might have assumed Elias would be the one prone to henpecking and worrying. Yet it was Cade, the product of a home as cold and distant as Elias' had been warm and encouraging, who bore that particular mantle. Elias supposed it worked out for the best since he was the one most prepared for a relationship where someone nagged out of concern, stuck their nose in business that wasn't their own out of worry, and pestered because they loved. It also turned out, in a strange twist of fate, that Cade was the better cook out of the two of them as well.

Cade's attention turned back to his book. "Speaking of, how is your mom?"

Elias eyed him doubtfully. "You're telling me that she hasn't spoken to you?"

"Not recently."

Elias grunted, surprised. His mother had taken to Cade because she knew that in terms of motherly affection, Cade knew about as much as the desert knew rain. But aside from the fact that his mother hadn't learned much about Cade until after her last visit, Alexandra Cortez was a woman who poured love into any soul she took a shine too. That she would later learn more about Cade's childhood, in the months after their first meeting, had only increased her desire to smother Cade with love. The end result, between a private need for love on Cade's part, and Alexandra's refusal to take no for an answer, had been that she had taken on the role of a second, and maybe even primary mother figure for Cade.

"Surprised she's let you get away with it," Elias said as he stood up.

Cade snorted, turning a page. "She's been letting you get away without calling her."

"She doesn't dote on me like she does you."

"Jealousy?"

"Not even the slightest."

And there was none. If there was anyone in the world Elias believed could manage to love several people at once, it would be his mother. Alexandra Cortez had spent much of his youth adopting any and all of Elias' friends and those of his siblings. That same desire to care had extended to over a dozen dogs and cats in the intervening years, and a few birds and other assorted critters as well. He still distinctly remembered the large monitor lizard she'd taken on for about six months until a new owner, vetted by his mother, had come along.

With that, Elias walked around the big chair Cade had made himself at home in. Without thinking about it, he ran his hand through the man's hair, tousling it. As expected, Cade grunted at him in annoyance, but said nothing as he continued to read. It was meant both as a show of affection, but also to irk Cade, who was oddly touchy about his auburn hair that he never believed cooperated no matter what he did with it. Elias was probably the only person, outside Cade's numerous sex partners, who could get away with touching the man's hair.

Stepping through the small archway that would bring him into the main hallway, Elias made his way to the bathroom at the end of the hall. The only other doors were the one to his left, which led to his bedroom, and a closet. Much like the rest of the apartment, the bathroom wasn't terribly big, but that probably had a lot to do with the huge tub he'd had cleared to be installed. The only reason he could think of as to how he got away with it was because the building manager was either just easygoing, or he really liked firefighters.

After having gone to the bathroom and soaked his face with enough cold water to wake himself up completely, he stepped back into the hallway. He glanced through the archway once again, unsurprised to find Cade still curled up in the chair reading diligently. For all his active, restless energy, few things could engross Cade and keep him still for hours at a time like a book.

Elias stepped into the small dining room, equipped with a whole two chairs around a small table, and into the kitchen. It only took opening the humming fridge for him to remember that he didn't actually have anything worth preparing. There was a jug of milk, a drawer full of cheese, but little else save for deli meat. Grunting, he closed the door, and glanced around the cabinets, hoping he might realize there was something else waiting for him. His slowly awakening mind reminded him that there was nothing, and would be nothing until he dragged himself to the store. He let out a groan.

From the living room came Cade's wry voice. "So, I'm guessing me ordering us something earlier was a good plan, then?"

Elias perked up at that. "You ordered food?"

"That Thai place you like so damn much."

Elias hadn't felt very hungry when Cade had insisted he ate. However, just the mention of the Thai place a few blocks over was more than enough to send Elias' stomach rumbling in sudden desire. Few places could manage the spicy-sweet combination that reminded Elias of the Mexican cooking his father had loved so much while Elias was growing up and yet was somehow different. Strangely, no Mexican place in Port Dale managed to assuage that nostalgic urge in Elias quite as well.

"I won't say you're a lifesaver," Elias began.

"But you'll be thinking it quite loudly," Cade finished.

Elias leaned into the living room, smirking down at Cade. "Maybe. Maybe not."

Cade looked up, bright hazel eyes gleaming with amusement. "Or, you know, definitely will."

"Probably means I should pick the movie tonight, then?" Elias asked, raising a dark brow.

"Weren't you about ready to pass out a few minutes ago?" Cade asked.

Maybe he was, and maybe he wasn't. But it was obvious Cade was wide awake, and had already taken steps to take care of Elias, even if it did come in the form of a little bit of bullying. Plus, it had been almost a week since the last time the two of them had done anything together. Elias had had his nap, and he wasn't willing to throw away the few hours they might have to chill by sleeping it all away after gorging himself.

"Eh, something spicy and fun sounds good," Elias said.

"We talking food or movie?"

"Yes."

Cade snorted. "Sounds like a plan."

Plus, Elias knew Cade had seen his mother earlier that day. If there was ever a person who needed some sense of normalcy, of comfort and warmth, it was Cade after a meeting with Pamela.

Elias chuckled. "Sounds good to me too."

ONCE MORE, he found himself having to grope at the fuzzy edges of his thoughts to realize what was happening. The TV was still going, but it wasn't quite as loud as he remembered it being. It was obvious he'd fallen asleep again, stuffed full of delicious Thai food and an easy to watch and not get absorbed into, movie. There was a pleasant enough weight on his lap at the moment, and he had to work to drag himself out from the haze of sleep that wanted to pull him back down.

Cracking open his eyes, he blinked at the bright light

coming from the table beside the couch. The weight on his lap turned out to be Cade's legs stretched comfortably across Elias' thighs. The other man had propped his back against the other arm of the couch. Apparently, he'd decided Elias had officially conked out for the night, and Cade was no more interested in the movie than Elias had been. Cade had dragged his book over to resume reading.

That Cade was fast asleep was a testament to how late it must have been. Elias fumbled his hand on the other side of the couch, picking up his phone. It was well past midnight, going on almost one in the morning. No wonder Cade had fallen asleep. The only things that could keep Cade up past eleven were a few drinks in his system, some good music, and a pretty girl who had his eye. The book must have been a good one, though, as it was still in Cade's hand, draped over his chest.

Elias' little bit of movement hadn't done much to stir Cade from his sleep, but Elias knew that the moment he moved the man's legs, Cade would be awake and alert instantly. It was the sort of speed to alertness that came in handy when you were sleeping in the station, and a call came in. Cade swore up and down he'd been like that his whole life. In reality, Elias had seen the man sleep deeply more than once, though no one else ever admitted to seeing it. Maybe it was just a product of their friendship, but it still felt kind of nice to have someone be so comfortable they broke their own sleep habits around you.

Grimacing at a sudden, urgent pressure at his waist, Elias knew he was going to have to wake the man up. Mindful of not startling Cade awake, he lay a hand over the man's thigh, giving it a light shake.

"Hey, Cade," Elias said, voice rough and low from sleep.

Cade's eyelids fluttered. "I'm awake."

31

"You are now, but I need you to get up," Elias told him. "Or at least move your legs."

Cade chuckled thickly. "Is that why you're copping a feel?"

Elias rolled his eyes, taking his hand off Cade's leg and slapping it lightly. "Keep dreaming pretty boy, now get up so I can piss."

"Mm, yeah, I'm kinky, but not that kinky," Cade admitted, pulling his legs back to let Elias up.

"Duly noted."

Finally extricated from the non-stop warmth Cade gave off, Elias stood up and made his way to the bathroom. From the living room he could hear the faint sound of shuffling and the sound of the TV going off. Elias had had Cade stay overnight enough times to know that the next stop would be, yeah, there went the door as Cade locked it and tested it. Next would come the kitchen where Cade would grab a bottle of water and down the thing in one go. The crinkling of the plastic bottle echoed down the hallway, and as Elias washed his hands, he heard the soft footfalls of Cade, making his way down the hall.

Elias stepped out of the bathroom, turning off the light behind him. His bedroom door was left open, and he walked in to find Cade sprawled on the right-hand side of the bed. The overhead light had been left off, and only the moonlight streaming in through the curtained windows illuminated the room faintly.

"Not the best looking bedmate I've ever had, but you'll do," Elias said as he pulled at his shirt.

Cade snorted, curling himself around a pillow. "I'm the best-looking thing you've had in this bed for months."

"You're the only other person I've had in that bed for months," Elias admitted as he dug out a pair of loose pants from the closet.

"Gotta get you a girl one of these days."

"I think you more than make up for it."

"True."

Cade had already managed to strip down and dress in a pair of loose shorts that he'd left behind. All that was left was for Elias to crawl into bed too. The bed was huge, with more than enough room for even Elias' bulky, long body to share the space without ever touching the bed's other occupant. It was precisely the argument he'd used for why Cade might as well share the only bed in the apartment, rather than trying to sleep on the couch.

It was certainly one aspect of their friendship that they kept to themselves. Cade's mother would have probably had a fit to think of her son sharing a bed with another man, even if it was as platonic as it got. The guys at the station would have been just as bad, though that would have been more ribbing than any sort of moral outrage. Only a few of their sex partners had ever known about it, well, and the last ex Elias had.

For the two of them, it was a perfectly normal and sensible thing. It wasn't like they were naked and cuddling up, whispering sweet nothings to one another. And maybe there was something nice about having someone to share the space with, in the most literal of senses. If Elias really thought about it, having Cade around most of the time, even at night when they'd ramble about stupid shit or talk serious, was far better than most of the company Elias had hosted in his bed before.

Cade grunted, interrupting Elias' drifting thoughts. "Fuck, I forgot. You busy on Saturday?"

Elias' eyes flickered open, narrowing suspiciously. "Don't tell me you're about to invite me to another one of your mother's parties. I'm not doing it again, Cade."

Cade laughed. "God, she brought that up today. I'd take you along for that shit just to piss her off."

"I know you would. Hell no."

"Well, it's not her party."

"But it's a party that I have no business being at."

Cade groaned. "Somewhere along the line today, I agreed to go to some cocktail party. And half the City Council is going to be there."

Elias couldn't help his laugh. "Which means a certain secret admirer will be there."

"Ugh. I think to be a secret admirer, you'd have to actually keep it a secret."

Elias grinned. "True, she's not very subtle."

Christine Hoffman had the distinction of being the youngest member of Port Dale's city council. She was also unmarried and not shy about expressing her desire to change that. Elias would admit she looked good, and despite being surrounded by a conservative and old school circle of men and women, she sure didn't act or dress like it. Honestly, considering her penchant for short skirts and blouses that rode just the right amount of low, he was amazed people like Pamela, who wouldn't be caught dead wearing anything remotely revealing, would have anything to do with her.

"You could always just bite the bullet and go out with her," Elias told him.

"Yeah, thought about that, then I realized that if I did that, I'd never hear the end of it. My mother would be over the moon and wouldn't stop trying to get me to go out with her again. And c'mon, you heard Christine, she doesn't want just a date," Cade protested.

"Oh right, that comment about wanting to 'tame' you," Elias said, barely managing to hold back another chuckle.

"Oh shut up."

"Think it involves a collar and leash?"

"Have you seen the boots that woman wears sometimes? I wouldn't be surprised if she doesn't have a whole room full of fun things to 'tame' me with," Cade muttered with a shudder.

Elias smirked. "And you want me there, why?"

"Because I need someone huge to hide behind."

"Aw, thanks, you really know what to say to make a guy feel special."

"Seriously, just having someone there, having *you* there, will make it easier to sit through. We only have to be there for like, an hour, maybe two. Then we can get our asses out, come back to one of our places, drink a six-pack, and shoot at each other."

Elias raised a brow. "Got something new?"

"Dude, do you remember Halo?"

Elias snorted, remembering his teenage years spent shooting his friends, and aliens on the old Xbox console. "Yeah, of course."

"They remastered it, and guess who bought it?"

"Hmm, so I have to endure one of your stuffy dinner parties," Elias began.

"Not mine!"

Elias continued. "And in exchange, I get beer and the chance to relive my teenage gaming years?"

"That about sums it up."

Elias grinned. "Well, I guess you do know how to say the right things."

"You'll go?"

"You've charmed the pants off me, Mr. Masters, how could I say no?"

"Thanks, Elias."

Elias smiled. "Anytime, buddy."

CADE

*T*ugging at his shirt collar, Cade looked around the crowd of well-dressed people nervously. The party had already been going for nearly twenty minutes, and he still hadn't caught sight of Elias. It wasn't like the man was hard to miss. He tended to tower over everyone wherever he went. Cade wasn't exactly short, managing to stand over six feet, but Elias was practically inhumanly tall. Even in the thickest of crowds, his best friend stood out like a sore thumb.

And he was *late*.

Trying to ignore his frustration and nerves, Cade grabbed a flute of sparkling wine as it passed by on a tray held aloft by a well-dressed waiter. Honestly, just once, he'd love to go to a party held by the people his mother knew that didn't require an entire ensemble that cost more than his monthly bills. Even as a boy, he'd hated being dressed up and paraded before the rich and snotty people his mother adored so damned much. It really didn't matter that he'd been doing it his whole life, he hated the feel of the suit collar around his neck.

"Like a frigging noose," he grumbled.

Even worse, he could see Christine circling back around to speak to him again. He'd hoped to avoid her for as long as possible, but she'd snagged him before he'd gotten more than a few feet through the door. The deep blue dress she'd chosen was adorned with the tiniest flecks of some glistening silver material Cade didn't know the name of. But he thought it was supposed to give the illusion of the night sky. She was, thankfully, without the power boots he'd mentioned to Elias. Still, her shoe straps wrapped tight around her ankle, and her heels clicked loudly on the tile floor of the high rise restaurant she'd reserved for the party.

Thankfully, he'd been saved having to talk too much with her. As the hostess of the little affair, Christine was expected to flit around and greet everyone who showed up. She had to make nice, hold a bright smile, and give everyone just a dose of attention to make them feel welcome. That meant she'd only been able to greet him, bat her long eyelashes at him, and fiddle with a carefully loosened strand of hair, freed from her elegant bun, before having to move onto the next person. Cade wasn't so foolish as to believe that was it, however, she would make her way around to him again.

A familiar voice rumbled from behind him. "Please tell me you aren't already drunk."

Cade whipped around, letting out a relieved gust of air. "Jesus, Elias, there you are."

How the man had managed to come through the door without Cade spotting him first was unknown. He was wearing the suit Cade had insisted on buying him, telling him that if he was going to drag Elias around to different functions for moral support, the least he could do was use part of his monthly allowance from his parents to pay for it. The dress shirt wasn't one Cade had bought though, a light blue that contrasted nicely with the man's deeply tanned skin, and brought out his already bright blue eyes.

"Well, don't you dress up nicely?" Cade asked, meaning it.

Elias smirked. "Yeah, this monkey looks good in a suit."

"Now all we need is to slap you with one of those little...organs, I think they're called. Then we can stand on the corner, and you can dance for change," Cade teased.

"As great an idea as that sounds, I think I'll stick to risking my life fighting fires instead, thanks though," Elias said, taking the flute of wine from Cade.

"Hey! Get your own," Cade told him, letting go of the glass easily.

"Maybe you should get us both another one," Elias offered as he tossed the contents of the glass back. "Hm, not bad. Won't lie, you rich people do know how to find the good stuff."

"For all the money they spend on it, it better be good."

"True."

"And could you *not* shove me in the same category?"

Elias winked at him. "So, I shouldn't bring up the monthly allowance?"

Cade scowled at him. "No, you shouldn't."

The allowance had been one of his father's rare victories over his mother. Pamela would have been perfectly happy letting Cade leave behind learning the family business, going to college, learning how to be a perfect little next in line for the Masters' fortune. David Masters, however, had over-ridden his wife, refusing to let any son of his live, as he'd put it, 'like a pauper.' So, Cade had been given a monthly allowance, more than he ever would have made a month as a firefighter, but with a few caveats. Pamela wasn't one to take something lying down. She'd managed to wiggle in a few requirements, which included his weekly meetings with his mother, and going to any function she deemed necessary.

She'd yet to enforce more requirements, but Cade had a feeling he was going to see some interference in his personal life in the near future. At twenty-seven, he'd yet to 'outgrow' his 'phase,' and he could sense his mother's growing restlessness about it. Even his father had been hoping Cade would lose interest in his lifestyle by the time he'd reached his mid-twenties. He was at least far more subtle about his disapproval. Cade figured it was only a matter of time before his mother decided a more direct route was necessary to get what she wanted.

Cade dreaded the day.

Elias frowned at him. "You okay?"

Cade blinked. "Oh, uh, yeah, sure, got lost in thought for a minute there."

Elias' frown didn't ease. "Didn't mean to hit a sore spot."

"You didn't."

"Uh-huh."

Cade waved him off, not wanting to talk about it. There were very few people in what he considered to be his real life who actually knew much about his family. His name was unavoidable in the city since his parents had fingers in several different pots. It had taken him almost two full years of working at the station to escape the reputation of being a spoiled rich kid trying to slum. Elias was the only person outside his family who knew everything, and even then, Cade didn't want to have whole discussions about it.

Plus, it was enough to have Elias there with him. If there was anyone he would have chosen to have at his side at one of these boring and sometimes agonizing, functions it was his best friend. From the first conversation they'd had, Cade had found Elias comfortable. It had taken some of the guys at the station a while to come around to Elias. They tended to see the man's deep voice, which spoke little and usually only in short sentences, and the reserved, serious expression on his face, as aggressive.

Maybe Cade had just been wanting someone who was the calm to his frantic, the rock his emotional waves could crash upon. Or maybe he was just adding poetry where there wasn't any needed. He and Elias just...clicked. In over two years of friendship, they'd never done much more than bicker, and while they didn't always agree on everything, they knew how to get along with one another on an almost instinctual level. Honestly, if Elias had been a woman, Cade would have probably fallen head over heels for him.

Elias was the one who grabbed two flutes of sparkling wine from a passing tray. "So, seen Christine yet?"

"Yeah, she greeted me as soon as I came in the door."

"Greeted, or pounced?"

Cade took one of the glasses with a grunt. "Bit of both really."

Elias reached out, chuckling as he rubbed the middle of Cade's back consolingly. "Think you'll manage to get out of here before she comes for round two?"

"Not a chance in hell," Cade said as he took a drink.

Elias' hand drifted further down for a final pat before pulling away. "Well, you might not want to drink too much before she tries again. You might say something you'll regret."

"Yeah, I guess."

Cade's mind was more focused on the light, and brief touch from Elias. Physical contact between them had always come easy, though Cade had sensed it was strange for Elias in the beginning. While the larger man never put up a fuss if Cade wrapped an arm around him, laid against him, or any other number of casual shows of physical affection, it took him over a year before he was comfortable enough to do it himself. Then it had taken another few months for the affectionate gestures to stop feeling so forced and thought out. Elias' touch on his back just now had come without a thought, and Cade smirked into his glass as he realized how far along his friend had come.

He also wasn't going to stop drinking either.

Elias glanced at him. "Why are there no places to sit down?"

Cade rolled his eyes. "Apparently, Christine thinks people will enjoy themselves more if they're standing up. Probably thinks it'll encourage people to talk to one another more."

"Cue everyone standing around in huddles," Elias noted.

Which was true. The Marshalls were standing with the Windoms, the oldest of the rich and mighty had to stick together. Cade noticed the old blue-bloods were keeping an eye on the group of young, up and coming entrepreneurs standing on the other side of the room. These were the men and women who came from backgrounds that weren't generally all that different from Elias'. But through a combination of hard work, business acumen, and maybe a few dirty tricks along the way, were now considered part of the high and mighty. Though that was strictly in financial terms. The likes of the Marshalls and Windoms, who owned practically half the city and had been there since the founding of Port Dale, would never see the new blood as equals.

"I never said it was a good idea," Cade muttered.

"Every time I come to one of these things, I'm reminded of you comparing it to high school. And the more I come around, the more I understand it," Elias said with a chuckle.

Cade said nothing, glancing around for another flute of sparkling wine. Elias had the right of it, the wine really was *that* good. Didn't hurt that the bubbly stuff was beginning to fill him with a warm fuzziness that made the environment feel less restrictive. Maybe with a few more drinks, he might even begin to enjoy himself, wouldn't that be a strange turn of events.

Elias watched him with amusement. "What are the chances of you making a complete ass of yourself by the end of the night?"

Cade thought on it, signaling to another server with a polite, raised finger. "Somewhere between definitely and certain."

"Your mom really set you off the other day, didn't she?"

The question was as blunt as it was accurate. Leave it to Elias to understand just what it was nagging at the back of Cade's head. As he took another offered glass of sparkling wine, he smiled ruefully at Elias and turned his head away.

"Maybe we could talk about something other than my mother? That would be great," Cade said as he downed almost the entire glass.

Elias looked up, features tightening. "Then maybe we should talk about the fact that Christine is heading this way?"

Cade's eyes darted left and right, widened, and he groaned. "Oh fuck."

"You realize I'm not going to be able to help you, right?"

"Probably not, but that doesn't mean you can't be moral support."

"I'll hold you tight while you cry, good buddy."

Cade gave an ugly snort into his now empty glass. Despite being more expressive and energetic than Elias, Cade would hardly call himself emotional. He was about as likely to break down in tears as Elias' emotionally reserved ass was. The idea of the bigger man holding him close while Cade was overwrought with emotion was a strange one, strange enough to make Cade snicker as Christine approached.

The clack of her heels preceded her, and Cade forced a pleasant expression on his face as she neared them. Her eyes were wide with delight, and he didn't miss the hungry way her gaze swept over him. For almost a full year, she'd been trying to find a way into both his bed and his life. Cade had managed to avoid her so far, but the idea that she was getting friendly with his mother probably didn't bode well.

"Nice to see you're still here, Cade," Christine said, stopping in front of him.

As if he had a choice. "Of course, Christine, you know how I love to pop my head up every now and then."

"As you should. Pamela was very insistent that I include you tonight," Christine said.

"Yeah, well, as I said, I love showing up and being social. Obviously, the woman who raised me would know."

He could actually feel Elias stepping back away from them. Cade didn't blame him. Christine wasn't exactly making an effort to even acknowledge Elias' existence, and his friend couldn't exactly save him either. At least when the night was all said and done, he could rely on Elias to be there when he needed someone to complain to.

It was only then that her eyes darted over Cade's shoulder toward Elias. For a moment, he thought she might actually speak to him and make it a three-way conversation. When he watched her gauge the distance between Elias and them, however, his heart sank.

"I would greatly enjoy seeing more of you," Christine said lightly.

"Well, with the schedule I keep, it's difficult to make too many social engagements," Cade hedged.

Christine's dark eyes flashed in amusement. "True, true. I've had several things passed my way that say just how exemplary a job you've been doing. It's always impressed me how you've been willing to forgo all the trappings that come with the family name to...fight fires."

Cade smiled, not liking the sudden and pointed change in topic. "Well, you know, not everyone aspires to inherit the family business. I admire what my family has done for themselves, but my home is at the station."

She reached out, taking a glass from an approaching waiter. "As I said, it's impressive."

"It's nice that you think so," Cade replied casually.

Why did she look like a spider going for the kill?

"And as I said, between that and...other factors, I would like to amend my previous offer for you and me to spend more time together. After all, considering my work with the various stations throughout the city, I think we could see eye to eye on a great many things," she explained, cocking her hip evocatively.

"Ah, you do, do you?" Cade asked casually, now finally sniffing out the underlying threat he'd always feared would show up one day.

"I do."

Cade scrambled to find a way to put her off. The last thing he wanted was to date her. Either their relationship would fail and he'd find himself at odds with the woman who dealt with the station's budget and policy, or he'd be stuck with a woman who reminded him of his mother in too many ways for him to be comfortable. The only option he had was to find a viable excuse to continue avoiding her on an intimate and romantic level at all costs.

Christine raised a delicately trimmed brow. "And seeing as how you find yourself unattached, I find myself still interested and invested."

There! If he could use that. It wasn't like he was actually seeing someone, but he could use that all the same, right? Hell, he could just throw out a name and call it that.

"I am seeing someone," Cade said in what he hoped was a believable tone of regret.

The girl, Julie, popped into his mind as Christine cocked her head.

"Really? Color me surprised, your mother seems to believe you're...unattached."

"Well, she doesn't have to know *everything* about me, right?"

"Curious. The invitation included a plus one, and yet you...didn't? I would have thought you'd use these social engagements as a way of showing off," she continued with a faint curl of her lip.

Shit, she was right. If there was ever a way that would guarantee Christine would leave him alone, lest she be seen as some sort of man stealer in front of her peers, it would be to bring his current girlfriend with him. His mind raced, picking excuses and discarding them instantly. The invitation had come early, so it wasn't like he could say this nonexistent girlfriend didn't have time to make plans. Sickness? Too easy. Family emergency? Even worse.

"I did!" Cade heard himself blurt.

Christine blinked, expression blank. "You...did?"

Her eyes shifted over Cade's shoulder again, and at that moment, he realized both what she was thinking and where his panicked brain had leaped to. Cade turned on one heel, grimacing once his back was to Christine, as he caught sight of Elias staring down at him with a stony, unreadable expression.

"Isn't that right?" Cade asked, praying his friend would help him.

ELIAS

Of all the things he might have guessed would come out of Cade's mouth, the sudden gambit proclaiming them a couple was not one of them. As a matter of fact, Elias would have placed it on the list of top things Cade would *never* say. From the utterly blank expression on Christine's face, it seemed Elias wasn't alone in being knocked off-balance by Cade's announcement.

"Yeah, right," Elias said, thinking he deserved an award for how unbelievably casual his voice sounded.

Then again, a proper actor would have known what to follow up with. Instead, Elias stood there, feeling foolish as he held onto his half-drunk glass of sparkling wine, staring at Cade and Christine. Relief had flooded Cade's features, but Christine was still looking at them as though they had just pissed in her prize fern.

She recovered quicker than Cade did, however, drawing herself upright once again. "Well, this is...a surprise. I hadn't realized you were so...diverse in your tastes."

Elias knew Cade well enough to know the man's tastes could definitely be called diverse, but not when it came to gender. He almost felt bad for Christine, who seemed to be fumbling for the right thing to say now that her latest attempt to get with Cade was recoiling hard in her face. It was more that he was bewildered as to why Cade had launched into using Elias as a shield all of a sudden. It wasn't like the conversation between Cade and Christine had been all that weird. To his credit, Cade was still looking at Elias with wide, startled eyes, as though he too was wondering what the hell he had just said.

Cade whirled around, taking a step back toward Elias. "Well, it was a surprise for us too."

That was putting it mildly.

Cade reached back, his hand fumbling over Elias' arm and then finally settling over the middle of his back. "But hey, take what you get, right?"

Christine continued to stare at them with wide, curious eyes. "And...just how long has this been going on?"

"It's recent," Cade spat out hurriedly.

Elias tilted his head, not sure if he should return Cade's touch. "Very recent."

"But still important," Cade added on.

"Of course," Elias said.

Finally deciding he had to do *something*, Elias let his free hand come down to rest at the base of Cade's neck. Putting a benign smile on his face, he flexed his fingers, gripping the muscles of Cade's neck and shoulders affectionately. Elias wasn't sure what was stranger, the fact that it felt natural to do it, or the fact that Cade didn't grow even more tense at the touch. Then again, the man's muscles were rock hard, maybe he just couldn't get tenser.

Christine's eyes continued to sweep over them, darting and landing with seeming abandon. Yet Elias was left feeling more evaluated than the last time he'd had an Xray. She might have been a rich socialite, but Elias had no doubt the woman was sharp. It was obviously bizarre for Cade, a man who had a lifetime of dedicated heterosexuality, to suddenly claim he was dating another, completely straight man.

What the hell had Cade been thinking?

A smile finally graced her features, though it did nothing to assuage Elias' nerves. "Well, what a surprise and a pleasant one at that."

"It uh, doesn't bother you?" Cade asked nervously.

Was that hope in his voice?

Christine fixed a stray lock of hair, tucking it behind her ear. "Bother me? I would be lying if I said I wasn't a little surprised considering...well, all the same, I'm not some member of the old guard. I'm a child of the 21st century, after all. I think it's absolutely wonderful that you've discovered this new...side of yourself."

Her words were bright, and her smile just as much so, but Elias felt a squirming in his gut as she spoke. Though she wasn't exactly glaring at them, he didn't like the thoughtful way her eyes darted between him and Cade. Though he couldn't prove it, he was sure Christine knew Cade had been lying out of his ass and that Elias was backing him up.

Cade, however, seemed to relax the tiniest amount. "Right, of course. I suppose I shouldn't have doubted you for a second."

She shrugged her thin shoulders lightly. "No offense meant, no offense taken, right?"

"Of course."

"And in these current days, even with all the acceptance flooding in from all angles, I imagine it was a very difficult realization to come to."

"Uh, yeah, it had its moments."

Christine turned her gaze to Elias. "And you?"

Elias blinked. "What?"

"Was it difficult for you?"

"Oh. Well, you know. It was a little strange at first, yeah. Took some getting used to, wrapping my head around it."

"Of course."

"But when you've got something good, you go for it, no matter how strange it might seem at first," Elias continued, realizing he was babbling.

Christine nodded, eyes wide with interest. "I can imagine. After all, before all of this, you both were...perfectly heterosexual, right?"

"Yeah," Elias said.

"Yes," Cade agreed.

"So I can only imagine how very strange and even...melodramatic getting to this point would have been," Christine continued.

"Well, as I said, it had its moments," Cade said slowly.

Yeah, this was not a woman who was fooled by Cade's story. Neither Elias nor Cade were willing to get into too many details from the looks of it, though Elias could only guess at his friend's reasoning. Elias wasn't a liar by nature, but he knew enough about it to know it wasn't a good idea to make up too many details. The best way to keep to a lie was to stay as close to the truth as possible. That way, you didn't mix up too many of the fake details and end up caught. The problem was, none of what they were saying was even remotely close to the truth, and Elias had simply said the first thing that sprung into his head, the things that made the most sense.

"I'm sure there's plenty of stories you both have to tell," Christine continued, her tone encouraging.

And there it was, she wanted details.

Elias cleared his throat. "Well, no offense, but it's only recently that we've got into...this. Talking about it so freely in a room full of strangers is a little...weird, for me."

It was a cop-out, he knew it, Cade knew it, and he'd bet

every dollar in his bank account she knew it too. Still, he was hoping to appeal to the sense of propriety that Cade swore up and down was bred and drilled into every rich kid's existence, at least the high society ones.

Christine winced delicately. "Of course. This all must have been so unbelievably difficult for you both, but it does seem to have ended well for you, hasn't it?"

"Yeah," Elias said.

She grinned. "Well, then that's all that matters, doesn't it? I apologize if I seemed too intrusive. This was a surprise, and I'm afraid I lost my manners. Of course, you don't want to talk about your personal affairs in front of a room full of perfect strangers."

Elias gave her a smile. "Well, thank you for understanding."

"I suppose tonight was a good thing then. After all, I'm sure you'll be expected to accompany Cade to all sorts of engagements in the future. Oh, speaking of engagements…"

Cade held up a hand sharply. "One thing at a time, Christine."

"Of course. Ah, love, its joy is just so…infectious. Forgive me," she said with a light, tittering laugh.

Before they had to decide how they were going to respond to that, a soft voice called for Christine from near the back of the room. Elias turned to see the group of 'new money' raising their hand, politely but insistently motioning her over. When Elias turned back to face her, the smile had frozen on her face.

"Ah," she sighed. "The life of a hostess. It never ends."

"Maybe the next party you can enjoy yourself a little more by not hosting it," Cade offered.

"Now there's an idea. Will you two be staying long?" she asked.

Cade answered hurriedly. "We haven't made up our mind. We can't screw with our sleep schedules too much."

"This from the man who liked his weekend outings," Christine teased with a wink.

Cade jabbed a thumb at Elias. "Well, we can't screw with *his* too much. Do that, and he'll not sleep right for days, and no one wants to see that."

Elias frowned at him. "Hey."

Christine laughed, handing her now empty glass to another server. "Well, it's nice to see that you two are managing, and it's sweet of you to care, Cade. If you do leave before I see you both again tonight, be sure to at least stop by and say good night."

Before they could say anything else, she raised her hand to the group waving her over and marched away. Elias watched her long strides as they took her out of hearing distance. A glance around told him no one was near enough to hear him either, not if he was quiet.

"Other engagements?" Elias hissed quietly.

"Now is not the time for that," Cade muttered.

"Dating?" Elias persisted.

"Definitely not the time for that."

"Then when, *honey*?"

Cade winced. "Look, let's just get through the next few minutes of this party, pretending we're happy and having a good time. Then we'll slip out the door when Christine's distracted, and we can go back to your place, and you can yell at me."

Elias didn't want to yell at anyone, but he sure as hell wanted some answers. Christine had been far too interested in getting answers out of the two of them, and her eyes had been far too bright for Elias' liking. He didn't know Christine personally, only what few things Cade had told him, and that she was apparently on good terms with Pamela. Add all those things together, and he couldn't rid himself of the nerves jangling away in his guts.

Cade took a deep breath, closing his eyes. "Just...let's get through this. Then we can get it over with at your place, okay?"

"Yeah, yeah," Elias agreed, left with the sinking feeling that it wasn't going to be over quite that easily.

* * *

CONSIDERING how intent on them Christine had been, leaving had been a remarkably smooth process. Elias had honestly expected the woman to hunt them through the party, and ambush them the moment it looked like they were trying to leave. Then again, maybe he shouldn't have underestimated just how tricky Cade could be when he was forced. Elias waited until Cade had given the signal, and the two of them had simply walked out.

He might have anticipated that leaving would be the hard part, but he hadn't quite been expecting how awkward the ride back to his apartment would be. While he knew Cade was probably upset about the entire thing, Elias hadn't been expecting the total silence that filled the car as Cade drove them back. Even the radio had been turned off, leaving them to sit in the car with only the sound of the engine and the occasional noise from outside coming through the window.

Christ, was Cade pissed at him?

It was a thought that scratched at the back of his head. Digging deep into his mind as Cade parked the car and they slipped out. Elias wasn't sure what the hell Cade could be mad at him about. Then again, he hadn't exactly expected the night to go the way it had either. He'd also never known Cade to give anyone the silent treatment unless he was pissed at them, choosing to keep his lips sealed rather than risk saying something he might regret in the heat of the moment.

It was only when the door of his apartment was closed behind him that he watched as Cade's shoulders slumped, and a harsh breath escaped him. Cade's bright eyes turned to him, openly searching Elias' features with something that Elias could only call hesitation.

"Alright, let me have it," Cade said.

Elias frowned. "What?"

"Let me have it. I just told Christine and probably anyone that was listening that not only were you not as straight as you actually are but that you're dating me. I lied to save my own hide, so let me have it," Cade said.

Elias hesitated, understanding what had been wrong the whole time.

Elias snorted. "You think I'm mad at you."

"Um, aren't you?"

"Shit, I kept trying to figure out why you were so damn quiet on the ride over here. I even started to think I'd done something wrong to piss you off."

"Piss *me* off? What the hell would I have to be pissed at you for?"

Elias shrugged. "Fuck if I know, but you're normally only quiet when you're sleeping, watching a movie, reading, or pissed off at someone."

Cade opened his mouth, frowned, and then grunted. "Okay, that's fair. Fuck you for calling me out like that, but that's fair."

Elias pulled his suit jacket off, tossing it over the back of a dining room chair. "Go sit down and take a breath. I'm not pissed at you. I'm just going to get us some beer."

Shaking his head, he made his way into the kitchen to do just that. No wonder Cade had been practically mute the whole way home. The idiot had been waiting for Elias to lose his cool, which was funny in its own right. Despite Elias apparently looking mean and being too quiet for other people's comfort at times, it was Cade who had the temper. If there was anyone who was at risk of blowing a gasket and yelling, it would have been him.

Elias returned, twisting the cap off one and handing it to Cade. "Here."

Cade looked up from where he'd slumped in the plush chair. "Thanks."

Elias took the cap off his own and flopped down onto the couch. "Can't believe you thought I was pissed."

"I mean, you'd have every right to be pissed. I pulled you into it."

Elias snorted. "Man, I've been pulled into your shit since we became friends. That's just how friendship goes."

"Well, you certainly know how to make it sound so beautiful and poetic. You should write inspirational posters about friendship."

Elias smirked. "Might not be pretty, but it's true. Being friends with people means going through their shit just like they go through yours."

"Well, that's a little better."

"I try. And for the record, I'm not pissed about what you said."

Cade snorted. "Seriously?"

Elias placed the bottle between his legs with a light laugh. "I mean, I wasn't expecting it, and you surprised the shit out of me. But, if the past couple of years of people thinking I'm gay for you didn't bother me, people we see every day pretty much, why would I care if some strangers think the same thing? Plus, there are worse things than being known as the guy dating you."

"Hmm, worse things, huh? Like having cancer?"

Elias rolled his eyes. "Being known as your boyfriend isn't an insult."

And with that attempt at self-deprecating humor shot down hard, Cade lapsed into silence once again. Belatedly, it occurred to Elias that maybe he had gone a little too far in trying to reassure his friend. A strange, awkward silence fell between them, and Elias realized they weren't normally the type for kind words or reassurances. Their friendship was based more in just being there for one another, being someone to talk to and ultimately rely on to always have one another's back. Of course, there were the casual displays of physical affection, which after two years, felt as natural to Elias as their conversations.

Was it weird that he'd changed the script suddenly? Or was he just making himself feel weird about it because the whole situation was just plain weird?

Elias shook his head, knocking the thoughts away. "So, I do gotta ask, what the hell made you say it?"

Cade sighed. "Didn't you hear her?"

Elias grunted. "I was standing like, two feet away, I heard her. So what?"

"All that talk about wanting to spend some time with me."

"That's normal."

"And talking about the station and all that."

"Right, she does deal with our station, along with all the other ones."

"Elias, I've grown up around people like that, I know what she meant."

"Okay, well, forgive this poor kid who doesn't understand subtlety."

Cade scowled at him. "Don't."

Elias grinned. "You're still going to have to explain it to me."

"She was...threatening me without actually threatening me."

Elias frowned. "So like...your job?"

"Or maybe the station, I don't know. She's a woman who likes to get what she wants, and she's got...a lot of power. If she wanted to make my life hell, she could. And she could make it hell for the station too if she wanted. There's always something she could find to put pressure on the chief, and inevitably, on me. I may not be one to play the game, but I know it when I see it. She was trying to put the screws on me, pushing me to give in to be with her, even if that meant threatening what I love most," Cade said, bitterness heavy in his voice.

"Are...are you sure?" Elias asked. It wasn't like he didn't believe Cade, but Elias hadn't got that feeling at all from what she'd said.

Cade looked up, giving him a weak smile. "I know these people Elias, I know how they work. She wouldn't be happy unless she had a good reason to leave me alone."

Which only left the other question to be asked. "You know she's not going to let this go, right?"

"Caught that did you?"

Elias laughed. "She was uh, pretty persistent. Didn't seem like she was willing to bite quite yet, but knew she was trapped into looking like she did."

"Yeah, I don't know what she's got up her sleeve, but you could see the wheels turning in her head. She's not done with me quite yet, and I just hope it doesn't get too bad."

Cade's whole adult life had been spent trying to separate himself from the life he'd come from, even though he was bound to it through his parents and their financial allowance. Elias wasn't totally sure that Cade was on the money about Christine's original intent. Still, he knew the woman wouldn't give up, and she probably would be livid if she found out he had lied to her too.

Elias leaned forward, gripping Cade's thigh and giving it a squeeze. "Hey, don't worry too much about it."

"Uh-huh," Cade said, but still took hold of Elias' wrist and squeezed it back.

"You'll figure it out, and I've got your back, you know that."

"I do."

"Good. Then stop worrying about what *might* happen, you'll only drive yourself crazy. Instead, focus on what we're here for."

"Uh, getting drunk?"

Elias grinned, eyeing the TV. "Getting drunk and playing video games."

Cade's eyes widened. "Oh shit, that's right! Fuck, let me load it up, man...perfectly timed."

Elias chuckled, letting go of Cade's warm leg and sitting back on the couch while the other man hopped up excitedly. As much as he was glad that Cade was so easily distracted, he still couldn't shake the uneasy feeling in his own guts. He didn't need to read Cade's thoughts to know his friend was afraid that things weren't quite over.

And Elias agreed.

*N*either a good few hours of drinking and gaming with Elias nor a handful of hours sleep was enough to shake the nerves jangling around in his head. Cade had barely managed to swim to consciousness before the events of the night sank into his thoughts once again.

"Ugh," he grunted, rolling out of Elias' bed as gently as he could.

Elias, thankfully, didn't stir as Cade's feet hit the floor, and he pushed himself up. His friend had practically passed out the night before. It was a testament to how tired he was normally, and to how willing he'd been to stay up and hang out with Cade to keep him distracted. It was only when it became evident that Cade couldn't keep his own eyes open that Elias had finally announced that they needed to go to bed.

It was those little things, moments where Elias showed who he really was under all the quiet stoicism, when Cade thought his friend truly shone. Not once had Cade found himself ever wondering where his friend stood, or doubting if he could depend upon him. And the thing was, Elias wasn't afraid to speak up when it counted. Whether it was to tell the guys at the station to piss off when they were being bigger dicks than usual, or like the night before, refusing to let Cade insult himself when maybe, just maybe, Cade had meant the self-denigration.

How could he not? It had been stupid to panic at Christine's questions, at her repeated attempts to date him. Even worse, he shouldn't have dragged Elias into it. He shouldn't have been surprised that Elias wasn't pissed about it. For one, he was definitely the sort who would have, and indeed had, shrugged off the idea that he might be into guys. And Cade couldn't help an amused smirk at the fact that Elias thought that being 'accused' of dating Cade wasn't an insult.

"What're you doing?" Elias grunted suddenly, eyes still closed.

Cade froze, realizing he'd been standing at the end of the bed, watching his friend sleep. Heat flamed in his cheeks, and he was suddenly very glad Elias had decided to keep his eyes closed.

"Zoning out," Cade said hurriedly.

Elias gave another characteristic grunt, rolling onto his back. "That time?"

Cade nodded. "Yeah, figured I'd hop in the shower and give you time to become a person again."

Cade himself had always been a fairly light sleeper. Adjusting to the demands of sleeping on shift and in the station had come easy to him. Yet, despite having done the job as long as Cade, Elias still wasn't quite as good at it. Sure, if he was napping in the station and the alarm went off, he was on his feet and ready to go as quickly as anyone else. Outside of that, however, the man woke slowly and took forever to come to full consciousness. Elias had always joked that it was his reboot process, where he would have to spend twenty minutes trying to come to terms with his existence and then more to remember his own name.

"Mmph, coffee?" Elias asked.

"I'll get it started," Cade promised, patting Elias' blanket-covered foot.

And just like that, his somber mood evaporated. Maybe other people might think it strange that he and Elias spent so much of their free time together. And they probably thought it even stranger that two heterosexual men spent their shared nights in the same bed.

Honestly, he'd prefer to wake up in the same bed as Elias than he would most of the women he took home with him. That had been an odd realization the first time he'd had it over a year and a half before. But since then, Cade had come to realize it was true and to accept it happily. Sure, they weren't fucking each other, but it really was nice to just have *someone* there to wake up with, to have the companionship in the evening and in the morning. They knew each other's habits inside and out, and there was a comfort in that.

As though showcasing that very fact, Cade took the cold gallon of water out of the fridge, rather than use the tap where he'd generally get the water for his own coffee. After having made Elias' coffee enough over several months, he didn't even have to put much thought into the water to coffee ratio. Cade had always thought he liked his coffee strong. That was until he'd had Elias' coffee for the first time, which was so thick it could have probably been classified as sludge.

Just as Cade's finger hit the button to start the brewing process, he heard the bathroom door close gently. Sighing, he leaned against the counter and waited until he heard the flush, followed by the sink's running water. He listened further, waiting to see if Elias had forgotten what Cade had said, as he was prone to doing in the morning. To his mild surprise, he didn't hear the shower come on, and instead, the bathroom door opened quietly, spilling light into the hallway.

Smirking, Cade took a bottle of water from the fridge and made his way back to the bedroom. Elias sat at the end of the bed, staring at his lap and rubbing the back of his neck.

"Coffee should be good to go in five," Cade told him as he opened the closet.

"Good."

"And I promise a max of ten minutes in the shower this time."

"Liar."

That brought a smile to Cade's face as he fished a change of clothes out of the small compartment in the closet he used for his stuff. Cade was a sucker for his morning showers. Which meant that sometimes he forgot that he probably should share the time they had in the morning so that Elias could have one as well. Then again, it wasn't his fault that Elias had somehow convinced his landlord to let him put in a huge tub with all the fancy workings on it that made a shower at Elias' place heaven.

The thing had extra jets for God's sake.

"Just come yell at me at the ten-minute mark then," Cade said as he closed the closet.

Elias grunted, and Cade took that as an affirmative as he swept off to the bathroom to get his day started.

* * *

As ELIAS SLID the car into the parking spot, Cade slipped out into the bright morning sun.

"You know, as much as I hate these morning shifts, at least the traffic isn't bad," Cade offered.

Elias stepped out, still clutching his huge travel mug of coffee. "I just wish everything, our shift, and the traffic could be a little bit later. Waking up at the god awful start of the morning will never get easy for me."

"How is it that I'm the party animal, but you're the one who wants to stay up late when you've actually had some decent sleep?" Cade asked.

"I never get decent sleep."

"I think they call that insomnia in some circles."

"Probably."

"Something you can go to the doctor for."

"Tried that, remember?"

Cade sighed, shaking his head. He, of course, knew that Elias' sleep problems had started long before they'd met. Something about the onset of puberty had sent the chemicals in Elias' brain haywire, and suddenly the man was having sleep issues left and right. His mother had tried to get it looked at, but after several different medications, different techniques offered up by sleep specialists, and even a few desperate herbal remedies, Elias had just given up.

"There's always changes in medical advancements. They might still be able to help," Cade offered as they reached the back door.

"Cade, I really do not need to hear it from you too," Elias grumbled.

"Fine, I'll just spill all my woes to your mom the next time she calls me."

"I will end your life where you stand, Masters."

Cade laughed as they entered the building, making the sound echo up and down the length of the hallway. The thing was, Cade might actually bring it up the next time he spoke with Elias' mom. Madeline was a good woman, who loved her son dearly, and still occasionally treated him as though he were eight years old. She also happened to adore Cade, which, while bewildering at first, was something Cade had inevitably given into. When it came to Madeline's love, you were held hostage by it until you gave in, or you just accepted it from the outset.

"Need to call her again," Elias muttered as they entered the mess hall.

"Oh yeah, it has been a while, hasn't it?"

"Talked to her a bit last night, which was why I was late."

"Oh. Shit, God, if I'd known that, I would have told you to be more late."

"And what, risk you saying something else to Christine? Yeah, right."

"You have no faith."

"Nope."

They stopped as they crossed the dining room, realizing how quiet the place had been. Cade turned to find Matt at one of the tables, reading what looked like the next in the series of werewolf warrior books he'd been engrossed in lately. Cade swore up and down he wasn't going to ask the man what it was about either. The last time he'd done that, Cade had ended up dropping several dozens of dollars on an eight-part series of books after Matt had lent him the first.

It was the other two, Davis and Keith, that drew Cade's attention. The two men were watching them warily, as though they were two venomous snakes who'd wandered into the house. Cade frowned at them, shooting them a questioning look. Before he could actually get the question out, Keith pushed back from the table, leaving his bowl of cereal and marching out of the room.

"The fuck?" Cade proclaimed.

Davis looked between Elias and Cade, brow furrowed as though he were thinking way too hard about something. After another confused paused, he also got up, albeit with more hesitance, and less anger brimming out of him as he followed his friend.

Cade looked at Elias. "The hell happened when you worked with them the other day?"

Elias shook his head. "I went on a call with Davis, not Keith. And nothing happened. It was a normal fire, didn't even take much to put it out."

Cade turned to the only other person in the room. "Yo, Matt, the hell is up their ass? Did you offend their delicate sensibilities by daring to say you were dating a guy again?"

Seriously, those two had to grow up. Davis wasn't too bad, though it was blatantly obvious to anyone with a working pair of eyes that he wasn't comfortable around Matt most of the time. Keith, however, always seemed to be a hair's breadth away from saying something nasty. The only thing that kept him in line was the fact that the rest of the station wouldn't have tolerated it. They were all full-grown men who had grown up with the understanding that it didn't matter where you stuck your dick, and Cade was almost completely sure Elias had privately threatened Keith once before.

Matt looked up, brow raised. "Seriously?"

Cade winced. "C'mon man, I wasn't taking a jab at you. I was making fun of them."

Matt's brow never lowered as he marked his place in his book. "Yeah, I'm aware of that. But that's not what I meant."

Cade looked at Elias, seeing his sudden frown. "What? What'd I miss?"

Elias' frown deepened, but before he could say anything, the chief's voice boomed into the room. "Kaidan, Elias, my office."

"Oh, Jesus, what'd we do?" Cade asked as he threw up his arms in exasperation.

Fire Chief Irons was not a man to be kept waiting, however. The man was built almost as big across as Elias, but on a body that was a few inches shorter than Cade. Normally he let the station go about its business without much inter-ference, doing his job without feeling the need to breathe down everyone's neck. His beefy neck was beet red, however, which was always a sure sign the older man was stressed.

"Now," Irons barked.

"Coming," Cade sighed.

They followed after him, with Cade glancing at Elias for a bit of help or an idea of what could be going on. Elias looked even more concerned than before, but other than that, Cade couldn't get anything else from the man. Right before they entered the office, Cade caught sight of Keith at the end of the hall, preparing to enter the garage. As Cade stepped through, Keith shot him a dirty look, which only irritated Cade further.

The Chief's office was, as per usual, bordering on a disas-ter. Despite the fact that paperwork had gone the way of the dodo for most places, Chief Irons still managed to have it heaped up all over the place. There was a computer, but it was buried under a few folders, and there were a couple of notepads littered around the base of the monitor. Thank-fully, the chairs he used to talk to people were free of any clutter, allowing them space to sit down without moving anything.

"Chief, what the hell is going on?" Cade demanded once all three of them were sat down comfortably.

Irons looked between the two of them, his gaze finally settling on Elias. "Something tells me our resident quiet guy has an idea."

Cade's head jerked toward him. "Elias?"

Elias' face spasmed into a grimace. "Last night."

Cade blinked, confused. Then realization hit home with the force of a fire truck slamming into him.

No. She didn't.

Irons nodded. "I see someone's finally getting it."

"Chief," Cade began to sputter out.

Irons ignored him. "It was real interesting, getting a call from Christine Hoffman last night. Normally she only calls me to talk shop, maybe get my opinion on a few things. She's a busy woman, so she doesn't really take an interest in much else."

Cade closed his eyes. No, she didn't, but she sure would when it came to something she wanted badly enough.

"So you can imagine my surprise when she called me to congratulate me on the 'diversity of my workplace' and the 'inclusion of minorities' in her little speech. Truth be told, I thought she was talking about Matthew and his boyfriend, or the fact that Elias here is only half-white," Irons said, motioning to the now stone-faced Elias.

Cade snorted. "Like she'd even know Matt exists. Don't even think she knew Elias existed."

Until Cade threw him in front of her.

Irons nodded. "I was half right. She was talking about Elias. But she was talking about you too. It's a good thing I was already sat down, or I would've needed to have me a hard sit when she informed me you two are a thing."

And there it was. God, Cade knew that was the only reason Christine would have had to call Irons after what had happened last night, but hearing it was still a punch to the gut. He'd never given it any thought that what he'd told her in a moment of desperation would have leaked out into the rest of his life. Sure, maybe it would affect his relationship with Christine, and keep her watching him closely, but this? This was too much.

"Told her she had to be confused. Cade here can't keep it in his pants when it comes to the ladies, everyone knows that. And while Elias ain't exactly strolling them through his door like an amusement park, ain't no secret that he's strictly for the ladies. Then she told me that you yourself told her that was the case, and Elias was there, agreeing with you."

Cade gritted his teeth. "That is what happened, yes."

Irons looked at Elias. "That right?"

"That's right," Elias said softly.

Irons leaned forward, clasping his hands before him. "So, I didn't say much to her after that. Just told her that we don't give a shit where you put your pecker on your off-times. Mind you, I said it in much nicer words, but it's also true. Thing is, I don't quite believe this story either."

Cade took a deep breath. "Look, Chief…"

Irons held up a hand, shaking his head. "And personally, I don't really care *what* the truth is. If you two are really together, like everyone 'round here has been saying for a couple of years now, that's your business. Just make sure you keep it off the clock. But like I said, I don't think that's what's going on here. What I *do* know, is that she's awfully interested in this here relationship she says y'all are having."

"Yes, yes she is," Cade agreed.

"And what I also know is, she ain't just tellin' me for my own good, and she really didn't call me up to congratulate me. She don't care about none of that, so long as we don't do nothin' around here that makes us look bad. So that tells me she's got a reason, and since you seem to know her so well, I'm thinking that reason is you, Cade."

Cade said nothing, taking the hint that he should keep his mouth shut.

"And on that note, I don't wanna know what the truth is. Frankly, it ain't my business. But I'm tellin' you right now, her interest in this makes me nervous. She didn't say nothin' outright, mind you, but it made me nervous all the same."

Cade gave him a humorous smile. "She's uh, good at giving you the feeling that what she says isn't what she means."

Irons nodded. "And that you know exactly what she means. So, if I'm wrong, and you two are an item, there probably ain't going to be a problem. But if this is some bull-shit, you two cooked up for whatever reason, and she finds out, there is gonna be a problem. Then y'all are gonna have a problem with me, understand?"

"Yes, sir," Elias said softly.

"Good. I needed you two to know the score now that it's lookin' like there's a game in session," Irons said, finally leaning back in his seat.

Cade forced a smile that felt more like a grimace onto his face. "Thank you, sir."

Irons snorted. "Don't thank me, but now ya know what's going on. And for the record, whether or not this is a real thing, you let me know if those two idiots out there make any trouble. Already threatened Keith a couple of times when Matthew joined up, and I ain't afraid to do it again."

"Noted," Cade said, pushing up out of his seat.

Elias was already in the hallway by the time Cade reached the door. It wasn't like he'd expected his friend to say much, but the knot of worry in his gut was tightening. Elias' expression gave nothing away as he nodded his head to the end of the hall, toward the locker room. Cade nodded, mind already racing to figure out what he was going to say as he followed after his friend.

Elias spoke first once they entered the locker room. "I knew this wasn't going to end quietly."

"I'm so fucking sorry, Elias. I didn't think she would...I mean to call the Chief," Cade rambled.

Elias shook his head, holding up a hand. "Don't. Stop fucking apologizing already. Jesus, Cade."

Cade straightened, feeling a little more embarrassed that he might have been overreacting. "Sorry."

Elias sighed. "That one, I'll let go. Listen, if she's really up to something, and I'm betting the chief is right, and she is, this isn't going to stop anytime soon."

"It's just going to get worse," Cade said somberly.

Elias kept his voice low. "Yes, yes it is. She's not going to stop until she's either satisfied we told her the truth, yes, 'we', not just you, or she catches us in a lie."

Cade smiled a little at the reminder. "Okay, so what do *we* do?"

Elias snorted. "I guess, for now, you and I are dating. Which means we gotta put up with the stupid shit from Davis and Keith most likely. And it also means we're gonna probably put up with more shit from other places. If we bail out now, she's gonna get the claws out, and the chief is gonna have our balls in a jar on his desk."

"Great imagery."

"The point is, she's not going to stop. Not until she gets *something*."

"So we just...date?"

"Pretend at it, and hope she either loses interest, or we can go on long enough and 'break up' at some point. Until then, we better get our big boy pants on and get ready to act really convincing. Because if she gets mean enough, she can cost us our jobs."

"Christ," Cade swore, knowing he was right.

"I said it last night, and I'll say it again. I'm in this, I made myself be involved the minute I backed you up, and I'm not gonna be pissed about that. So we both better be ready, because this shit is only just starting," Elias said with a grim expression.

"And boy, I can't wait to see what comes next," Cade muttered.

"Personally, I'd be more worried about when your mother finds out," Elias said, clasping a hand on his shoulder before walking out.

Cade stared after him, Elias' words sinking in.

"Fuck."

ELIAS

*D*espite having nearly three days to adjust to the news, Elias could see that Davis and Keith were still being stubborn jackasses about the entire thing. Considering how they'd acted toward Matt in the past, Elias wasn't too surprised. Yet out of the past three days, he'd spent two of them with Matt, who had also been acting noticeably quiet and distant from him.

It's not like Elias sought out people for conversation most of the time, unless they were Cade, but he liked Matt. He was a smart guy, and he was probably one of the most gentle people Elias knew. He never seemed to have a bad word to say for anyone, even when it came to the likes of Davis and Keith. He was also incredibly friendly, and usually, if he was alone with Cade or Elias, he would have no problem whatsoever in talking their ears off.

Elias frowned as he checked over the hose in the compartment of one of the trucks. Everyone else at the station had been a little weird too, but no one had been standoffish. Elias suspected they would need another couple of days before the jokes started up again, though this time with a 'we knew it all along' flair.

He glanced over at Matt, who was bent over, checking the other compartments with pursed lips. They'd been doing their checks for almost a half-hour, and Matt had said little to him except a quiet greeting as they'd entered the room, and that had been about it.

Elias didn't consider himself a confrontational person in either a gentle or aggressive way. If someone said something stupid in front of him, he had no problem speaking up, however. It was trying to approach a problem that didn't require an angry voice and a not so gentle 'fuck off' that he had a harder time with.

"Hey," he called, knowing they were alone in the garage for the moment.

Matt looked up, blinking away the thinking haze from his eyes. "What's up?"

"Can we...talk for a second?" Elias asked.

Matt's expression slipped into a faint grimace, but he nodded. "Of course."

Elias slipped the lock back over the compartment and faced him. "Like, can we talk about how weird things have been with you the past few days?"

"With me?" Matt asked.

Elias motioned at him. "I mean, c'mon, you've barely spoken a word to me since...since word got out."

Since the chief apparently decided everyone had to know about it. Elias still wasn't completely sure what the reasoning behind that decision had been. Either the man had been so dumbfounded by what he'd heard that he hadn't thought, or he wanted to make sure Elias and Cade both knew what the stakes were by ensuring everyone would be watching them. Not that it made a bit of difference, it's not like they would have been allowed to be a couple on the job anyway. Telling everyone at the station just made things too damn awkward.

Matt sighed. "I'm...I'm sorry. It's just been hard to wrap my head around everything."

"I don't understand. I mean, if there was anyone here that I would have guessed would have been okay with it, it would have been you," Elias admitted.

"Yeah, that's exactly what Trevor told me when I told him about it. But I guess I'm just as bad as the others," Matt said with a sad shrug.

Elias snorted. "Davis and Keith are being like that because they're assholes, especially Keith. You're not an asshole."

"I just...feel bad. I'm not trying to be an ass about this. It's just...weird."

"Yeah, it is a little weird, I'll give you that."

Elias couldn't help but wonder if he knew the reason. "Like, is this like...shit, I don't know, because of me?"

Matt cocked his head. "Wait, like...me being jealous?"

Elias winced. "Maybe?"

That earned a smile from Matt. "Guess it's kind of hard not to think that when everyone kept joking that you were right up my alley."

"A little, yeah."

Matt shook his head. "I mean, don't get me wrong. When I first saw you, my first thought was 'oh hello.' But it never went further than that. You're a good looking guy for sure, but more importantly, you're a good guy. I'm not jealous that Cade is dating you, though that's a sentence I never thought I'd say."

"Yeah, tell me about it," Elias muttered.

"I just...you guys have been doing this thing for a while, right?"

"Right," Elias said.

God, it was one thing to lie to Christine or to the chief, but he felt like shit for lying straight to Matt's face.

"So I guess, for me, I just...wonder why you didn't tell me. I mean, I would have been the guy to tell, right?"

"It was just..."

Okay, it was day three, and he'd finally found the person he couldn't tell the lie to. He would lie his ass off to just about everybody else, especially Keith and Davis, because the bastards deserved to be uncomfortable, but not Matt.

Elias drew closer, motioning for Matt to get closer as well.

"We're not," Elias muttered quietly.

Matt's eyes widened. "What?"

Elias explained about Christine and the party the other night. Then he had to explain what Cade had said, and how Elias had backed him up. Which had then snowballed into the chief finding out, deciding to tell everyone, and holding them to the unintended game that Christine was playing.

Matt's eyes were wide by the end, but he kept his voice low. "You're telling me, this whole thing is a lie?"

Elias glanced around, checking the doorway leading to the back. "Yes. One we shouldn't have told from the start, but now we're kind of trapped."

Matt whistled. "So now you guys have to...deal with all this shit because of it?"

"Something like that."

"Damn. If there was ever a reason to tell the truth, this would be one of them."

"Yeah, tell me about it. But we're stuck."

"If Cade and the chief are right about Christine, then yeah, you guys are. What are you going to do, though? It's not like you guys are like, actually into guys, so what? Pretend for months, years?"

"We're hoping it'll cool off in a few more weeks."

Matt snorted, shaking his head. "If she's as devious as Cade says, I think she's going to turn up the heat a little more before she's done."

"Yeah, so do I," Elias admitted.

Matt frowned up at him. "Why are you telling me the truth?"

Elias shrugged. "Because I hated lying to you. And honestly, if there's anyone who deserves to know, it'd be you. Felt weird lying to you about it."

"Because I'm gay?"

"That and I like you, you didn't deserve to feel like you were left out of the loop."

Matt beamed. "Well, that's something, at least."

"And uh, sorry for invading your sexuality to help my best friend avoid having to date a harpy."

Matt gave an ugly snort, clamping his hand over his mouth to contain his laughter. Matt shook his head violently, waving at Elias as though to tell him that was okay.

"You good?" Elias asked once Matt had calmed down.

Matt took a gulp of air and nodded. "Yeah, yeah I'm good. Whew, was not expecting that one."

"Well, I mean, it's true."

Matt shrugged, tucking his checklist under his arm. "It's okay, I don't take offense. You get out of a bad situation the best you can sometimes, just sucks that it's uh, backfired this time."

"Tell me about it."

Cade appeared in the doorway, frowning down at a packet of papers in his hand. "Hey Matt, someone's gotta do the school thing again."

"School thing?"

"Yeah, you know the place where all the screaming gremlins like to go?"

Elias snorted. "I believe people call them children."

"Noisy, disease-carrying, gremlins."

Elias rolled his eyes. Despite Cade's attempts to pretend like he hated kids, he was actually really good with them. Elias had a deep suspicion that Cade's attitude had more to do with the fact that Pamela was constantly annoying him to give her grandkids, within the bounds of an acceptable marriage that was.

Matt raised a brow. "And why should I be the one to do it? The kids love it when firefighter Cade shows up to tell them about fire safety."

"Because you enjoy it," Cade shot back.

Matt smirked. "Yeah, and so do you."

"Do not."

"Do too."

Elias rolled his eyes. "Children, behave."

Matt reached out and took the packet. "Fine, I'll take this time around, but you're doing the next one."

Cade's eyes widened. "But after you would be Elias."

Matt winced at Elias. "No offense, big guy, but you scare the kids more than you help them."

"Not one piece of offense taken," Elias told him.

Matt smiled warmly at him. "Good."

"Why is it that you can get attention from men and women for your looks, but somehow, you scare kids? This is crap," Cade pouted.

"Because full-grown men and women get turned on by guys who are big and scary looking, it's a thing. Kids aren't exactly into scary," Matt explained with a smirk.

"Always knew you were a freak," Cade accused.

"Only in the sheets. You can ask Trevor all about it if you want," Matt offered, turning his attention to the papers.

"I'm not asking your boyfriend about how freaky you are or are not."

"Shame, he might be able to give you some pointers."

"For what?"

Matt looked up with a raised brow. "With all the gay sex you're apparently having, despite never having had it before."

"Oh."

Elias shook his head. "Seriously, Cade."

Matt chuckled. "I'm going to look over this, see what they want me to talk about this time. You two get out of here before the chief finds something else for you to do. Or Cade says something really transparent again."

"Trans…" Cade began, watching Matt walk off.

Elias waited until Matt was gone, and sure enough, Cade wheeled around on him.

"You told him," Cade accused.

Elias shrugged. "Maybe I did. Maybe he deserved to know."

"Seriously?"

"He looked like a kicked puppy earlier because he thought we were keeping the relationship a secret from him. C'mon Cade, do you really think he's going to tell anyone?" Elias asked.

"No, probably not."

Elias slung an arm around his friend's shoulders. "Then stop worrying about it."

"Just admit you're a sucker for puppy eyes, and I will."

Elias bent down, smirking at Cade. "Is that why I became friends with you?"

Cade swatted at him. "And started dating me. Don't forget to include that when people ask what you saw in me."

"I think people expect me to say your smile or your ass."

Cade wrinkled his nose, twisting to look behind him. "I don't know, do you think you could say it was a good ass with a straight face?"

Elias smirked. "Straight face, huh?"

"Oh, god, no puns."

77

Elias laughed. "I think I can."

It wasn't like Elias was blind or unwilling to 'risk' his sexuality by noticing whether or not another guy was good looking. Elias had absolutely no problem understanding why women were so drawn to Cade. Auburn hair and twinkling hazel eyes were a good start, but Cade took care of himself, and always made sure to look his best when he went out in public. Though as Elias pointed out once, women seemed to like him more when he was sweaty, grizzled from a long night, and smeared with soot.

So yeah, he could say Cade had a nice ass, because he did.

"I would love to see that in action," Cade said.

Another sound brought his head up, and Elias spotted Keith standing in the doorway, having come from somewhere in the back. The man's dark eyes were locked on them, and as Elias watched, the man's upper lip twitched.

Elias smirked. "Yeah, Cade, I do think you have a great ass. It's one of your best features."

Keith's twitching lip lost the battle and finally curled upward. Without a word, the man turned on his heel and stomped back down the hallway. Elias had no idea why he'd come out to the garage, and he honestly didn't care.

Cade burst out laughing. "Oh shit!"

"Hey, you asked."

"God, that was amazing. He hasn't looked that pissed since that day you asked him why he's so worried about where Matt sticks his dick."

"Well! It's a good question."

"Yeah, but the way you put it made it sound like he was a little *too* interested."

"You ask me, he was a little too interested."

Chief Irons was the next through the door, and Elias groaned as the man headed straight for them. He knew they should have left, just like Matt had advised.

"Good, you two are still here," Irons began.

Cade winced. "Oh c'mon, chief, what'd we do *this* time?"

Irons glowered at him. "Shut up. Christine was in contact again."

"Oh, Lord. And here comes the left hook," Elias muttered.

Irons turned his glare on him. "You shut up too."

"Okay, and what does she want?" Cade asked.

Irons' expression turned pained. "It seems, in a continued effort to...applaud us for our inclusive environment, she is throwing a little party."

"A party," Cade repeated dully.

"A party in your honor. You're the guests of honor."

Elias stared at him. "Seriously?"

"Seriously."

"A party."

"The kind where people have fun, listen to music, have drinks. A party."

Cade interrupted with a groan. "Of course, and we're the focus. Which means even if we wanted to, we can't bailout."

Irons snorted. "Nope, not a chance. I've even switched your shifts around, so you have the weekend off. And, I even made sure to keep Davis and Keith here for the night of the party, so they have a reason to not go. See, everyone in the station is invited."

"And we can't have them turning it down and ruining the image she's trying to push about this station," Cade said with a sneer.

"Yeah, and you're goin' too," Irons added.

Cade snorted. "Like I didn't know that. God, just like her to not even tell us first."

Irons raised a thick brow. "Accordin' to her, she did. Should check your phone more often."

"You're always telling us to leave them out of sight!"

"Like that's ever stopped any of you."

Grumbling, Cade pulled his phone out of his pocket and unlocked the screen. Elias peered over his shoulder and watched him open the message. Not only had Christine sent the invitation, but she'd taken the time to pretty it up. The picture message was of a black background, popping with little stars and fireworks. To Elias' faint annoyance, the text on the picture invitation was swooping and colorful.

"Is that glitter font?" Elias asked.

"Yes," Cade said through gritted teeth.

Elias read it over. "Saturday."

"At...Pulse?" Cade said with a cock of his head.

"Gay club," Elias told him.

"And how do you know that?"

"If you paid attention when Matt talked, you'd have known that too."

"I pay attention!"

Irons grunted. "Right, so you boys will be there. Make yourselves nice and pretty, and put on a good show, will ya?"

"Chief," Cade whined in protest.

Irons turned and walked off. "Nice and pretty boys, smile for the nice lady who keeps us around."

"Goddammit," Cade muttered.

"When she's got us by the balls, she sure does like to twist and pull," Elias said.

"She's *evil*."

"But one we have to deal with."

Cade tucked his phone away. "Christ, two days. Two days and we're going to have to..."

Cade didn't need to finish. He sounded just as worried and confused as Elias felt. Who the hell knew *what* would be expected of them? Well, at least it was Cade, and not someone else. Elias could live with...whatever, so long as it was Cade.

CADE

*C*ade peered up at the pulsating neon sign that read 'Pulse' in rapidly shifting colors. "Well...that's bright."

Elias stopped beside him, wincing at it. "Maybe a bit too bright."

"Jesus," Cade muttered.

Elias' hand came to rest on Cade's lower back. "Breathe. We talked about this. Don't think too hard about it."

"And you won't worry about it too much," Cade finished.

And yeah, they had talked about it, many times in the past forty-eight hours. It was a wonder Cade hadn't manage to give himself either an ulcer or a migraine from how badly his nerves had been jangling around. Elias was right, though Cade personally felt it was easier said than done.

"How the hell are you so calm about this?" Cade asked for probably the thousandth time.

"Would it make you feel better if I said that I already had a few shots before you picked me up? And that I plan on drinking considerably more once we get inside?" Elias asked, the corners of his mouth twitching.

Cade slapped his arm. "You absolute dick! You've been telling me to be calm, and you've already pre-gamed?"

Elias chuckled, patting Cade's stomach. "We'll get you a drink as soon as we get inside, I'll even make sure they make it nice and strong for you."

Cade knew he was pouting, but he didn't care. "Fine, but it better be *really* strong."

"Anything for you."

Cade knew he was being teased, but the comment made him smile anyway. It wasn't quite enough to get Elias off his temporary shit list for cheating, but hey, it was a start. He considered himself mollified enough to be led into the club, paying for both their cover charges since Elias was apparently content to buy the first round of drinks.

Cade was pretty familiar with clubs, and he had to admit, despite the brightness of the outside, the inside was pretty nice. Against the far back wall was a line of semi-private booths for people to sit in. There were tables in front of them where the more raucous people could stand or sit on tall chairs to watch the people on the dance floor. The dance floor was much like the sign outside, lit up brightly from below by lights protected by the thick, transparent flooring. The bar was on the opposite side, where most people filtered to and trudged away from with drinks in their hands.

Cade groaned as he spotted Christine and the group standing in the booth area, with a few of them claimed by what looked like decorations. Elias' gaze was locked on them as well, though his face didn't shift from its typical stoicism.

"Right," Elias said, turning and making straight for the bar.

Cade couldn't help his soft laugh, hurrying after Elias so he wouldn't be spotted. He still had no idea what Christine was up to, or what she was going to put them through. What he did know was, he was probably going to need plenty of drinks to get him through the night.

Elias leaned over the bar to get the bartender's attention. "Gonna need two double shots."

"Of?" the amused looking man asked.

"Whatever won't kill us immediately but kicks like a mule."

"That I can do. Drinks?"

Elias glanced at Cade. "Beer?"

"Liquor. God, please give me liquor."

Elias turned back to the man. "Gin and tonic, and I'm betting this one wants a martini. Make that gin and tonic a double while you're at it."

"Someone's looking to get blasted early," the bartender chuckled.

"Just make it a dirty one," Cade said, feeling his nerves tighten.

"Can do."

The bartender was gone for only a couple of minutes, and the drinks in his hand were a welcome sight when he returned. Elias slid his card and ID onto the bar for the bartender to keep for the tab. He gazed down at the tall shot glasses sitting beside their drinks.

"What do you think it is?" he asked.

Cade shrugged, picking one of them up. "If it gets me drunk enough to stop freaking out, or at least not as much, I'll take it."

And at that, they clinked the glasses together and downed the shots. Whatever it was went down smoothly with the slightest taste of mint among the liquor. When it hit his stomach, however, Cade was left coughing as the fireball erupted from his guts. Elias only winced, but having seen the man drink before, Cade knew he wasn't being too dramatic.

"Jesus," Cade muttered, setting the glass aside.

"More like a horse than a mule, but it's got kick," Elias agreed.

Knowing he was washing down liquor with even more liquor, Cade plucked his martini glass up and took a deep drink from it. The large shot hadn't had a chance to get into his system just yet, but the jolt of taking it had been enough to clear his head a little. The martini was good too, and he hummed appreciatively as he took another drink.

"I'm so glad we ate before we came," Elias said with a smirk as he watched him.

"Says the man who already started drinking," Cade shot back.

"I also have more weight, and you've always been a lightweight."

"Bite me."

"If Christine has her way, I might have to."

Cade groaned, wishing the alcohol would start kicking in. The last thing he needed was to start thinking about what sort of show Christine was going to expect from them. If they had to walk around arm in arm, putting their hands on each other's back or whatever, he could live with that. Even if he had to sit in Elias' lap, it'd be weird to do it in public, but he could deal. But just how the hell was he supposed to get through doing more than that?

Well, at least it was just Elias, that would make it a little less weird.

Or wait, would that make it more weird?

Elias grunted. "We've been spotted."

Cade's head jerked up, and sure enough, Christine was looking across the room, eyes locked on the bar area. Her hand raised in a polite but enthusiastic greeting.

"I guess that's our cue," Cade said with a sigh.

Before Elias could say anything, someone sidled up to him.

Cade raised a brow at the thin man who barely came up to his chin. The man's bright eyes were turned up to Elias' serious features, and there was no missing the appreciative glint.

Elias watched him. "Yeah?"

The man didn't seem at all deterred by the neutral greeting. "I see you've got a drink, but maybe I can get you the next one?"

Cade snorted. "He's spoken for."

The man turned his gaze toward Cade, looking him over and smirking. "I mean, if you guys are down for sharing, I sure won't say no to you either."

"We're not, thanks though," Elias said before Cade could reply.

"Shame," the man said before turning to order.

"C'mon," Elias said, gently taking hold of Cade's elbow and leading him away.

Cade laughed. "Christ, is that what it's like in here?"

Elias shrugged. "Matt always told me that guys can be pretty...forward in clubs."

"I mean yeah, but…"

"But?"

Cade frowned. "Huh, guess I never thought about it. But I guess it makes sense. Usually, it's guys going after the girls. I guess when it's two guys, there's probably a lot less dancing around about it. That guy had no fear whatsoever, didn't even flinch. Just came right up to you and pretty much asked for your dick."

"Asked for yours too," Elias reminded him.

"For both of ours. Geez, gay guys really do have it pretty good."

Elias stopped. "Really?"

Cade thought about it and winced. "Well, with getting laid. Maybe...okay, not all the other stuff."

Christine approached them. "Hey! I'm so glad you two could make it."

"We had a choice?" Cade asked.

Elias snorted. "What he means is, we're so glad you're thinking of us. We know how busy you are, it's nice of you to take the time to celebrate something as small as our relationship."

"Oh, it was nothing," Christine said, laying a hand over her chest.

Elias shook his head. "No, credit where it's due. It's not often that our guys get to have something about their lives celebrated like this. I've already penned a letter to the council to thank them for their service, and how well they must be doing to have someone as dedicated as you with them."

Christine blinked. "Oh? Well, that's...very thoughtful of you. There's no need to go to the trouble, though. I do this because you two deserve the recognition."

"I can't stand the idea of you receiving none," Elias insisted.

Christine smiled. "Well, all the same, why don't you come and say hello? I'm sure you know the men from your station, but I have others I'd like you to meet too."

She turned away to return to the table, and Cade stared at Elias.

Elias glanced at him. "What?"

"You uh, play the game very well."

Elias shrugged. "Not really."

"Took the wind out of her sails. Do you really have a letter to send?"

"I might."

Cade grinned. "Oh, I'm sure they'd be *very* interested to know why she's so interested in this. Especially if she's using public funds."

"You think she's that dumb?"

"No, but who knows."

Elias winked at him. "You know, just because I'm stuck in her game doesn't mean I can't have a bit of fun myself."

Cade snickered. "Oh baby, I love it when you talk dirty to me."

"You sound like my ex. Next, you'll be asking me to pin you against the wall and have my way with you," Elias said with a chuckle.

Cade watched him walk off, unable to think of anything witty to say. That would mark the first time he'd ever learned anything about Elias' personal life in any degree of detail. Sure, he knew that Elias got laid once in a while, and he knew the man had a sex drive that would probably rival Cade's. The difference between them was that Cade was the one who actually sought out partners, Elias seemed content to be single unless he found someone worth his time. He'd never known that Elias...or did he actually know it? It wasn't like Elias had said he actually did like it rough, only that he asked.

Jeez, why did he even care?

Shoving the thoughts aside, he hurried after his friend to the group who'd assembled for them. Sure enough, there were a few guys from the station. Most of them were guys that Cade didn't see much, as they tended to work the opposite shifts to him and Elias. Matt was there, though Cade noticed he was alone.

Matt eyed the drink in Cade's hand. "Having fun?"

At that, Cade polished off his drink in one final gulp. "Just keeps getting better and better."

"I bet," Matt said, watching Elias as he talked to a couple of guys Cade didn't recognize.

"Christine brought in a few people from the other stations too. I guess she really wants to make a show of this," Matt added.

Cade looked at his empty drink. "We're going to be on display, aren't we?"

"If it makes you feel any better, I think the worst you'll have to deal with is a dance and maybe pucker up a little bit," Matt said.

"That's uh," Cade glanced over at the group, then shrugged. "Yeah."

Matt winced. "I know."

"Oh, god, can you...get me another one of these? Elias' name is the one on the tab," Cade asked.

Matt chuckled. "Considering the night, I think I'll get you this one, good buddy. Nice and strong, right?"

"The kind that makes me end up getting poured into a cab at the end of the night," Cade confirmed.

"Coming right up," Matt said as he slid from the booth.

It looked to be the only bit of peace and quiet he was going to get for a while. It took no time at all for Christine to descend on him immediately and begin chatting him up. Considering the majority of the talk was the typical back and forth he'd grown up with, he allowed himself to go onto autopilot. Matt had magically reappeared, with drinks for himself, Elias, and Cade, setting Cade's down in front of him before disappearing again.

Cade was really going to have to get that man a gift basket or something.

"Now, let me introduce a few people you might not know. This is Caroline and her husband Frank. They've both been at the forefront of campaigning for diversity and inclusion in the workforce of this city, and they were just delighted to hear about you and Elias," Christine said excitedly, motioning to two people who looked younger than him.

Yet, he did his duty and took each of their hands, shaking them with the most enthusiasm he could muster. A warm hand pressed against his back, and Cade stiffened.

"Making new friends?" asked Elias' deep, calm voice.

Cade shot him a grateful smile. "New friends for both of us."

"Oh good," Elias said, setting his glass down to shake hands as well.

Elias' hand never left his back, and Cade didn't bother to shake it off. Honestly, the more he let the warmth of the liquor settle through his system, the more willing he was to admit the touch was welcome. They were surrounded by people they didn't know, and those they barely knew, save for Matt. Slapped into a situation Cade himself had helped to create, it was soothing to have someone Cade knew he trusted utterly, so close to him.

As if sensing it, Elias never left his side, and never entirely removed his touch either. As Cade chatted away with the various people Christine insisted he talk to, Elias was always there. A hand upon his back when following close behind, a grip on the arm when Cade looked to say something foolish. At one point, Elias had laughed at something, placing his warm touch upon Cade's neck, distracting him from the conversation momentarily.

It didn't hurt that Cade was kept with a steady supply of alcohol. Both Elias, through the roaming servers that popped up, and Matt through a shrewd eye, made sure Cade wasn't without a drink. Once Cade realized he wasn't quite as tense and freaked out as before, he toned down just how much he was consuming. Despite his joke to Matt earlier, he didn't really want to end up a drunken mess in the back of a taxi. Elias' support was more than enough to get him through, especially now the alcohol was steadily pumping its way through him, making him laugh easier, talk smoother, and even almost enjoy himself.

"Cade?" Elias' voice pierced through his thoughts.

Cade jerked his head up. "Hm?"

It was then he realized that he'd zoned out once again and had missed a crucial part of whatever conversation was happening around him. There was no denying the fact that he'd mentally abandoned the conversation, however, as everyone at the table was watching him in amusement.

"Sorry, got lost in the forest of my thoughts," Cade admitted with a soft laugh.

Matt snorted. "Can't be that deep a forest."

Elias frowned. "Hey."

Matt raised his hands, looking somehow more amused. "My bad. I just meant that Cade is a very...straightforward person."

Christine chuckled. "Oh, he's just had a bit too much to drink."

Cade frowned. "I've had stuff to drink, but I wouldn't say *too much.*"

"Oh boy," Elias muttered just low enough that he couldn't be heard by anyone but Cade.

Christine beamed. "Well good. As I was just asking when we were going to see the two of you dance."

Cade's face blanked. "Uh, excuse me?"

"Well, it's a party for the two of you. I assumed I'd see you dancing at some point."

Cade snorted. "Who we dancing for?"

"Why, for each other, with each other," Christine said, leaning forward with a delighted twinkle to her eyes.

Cade turned his attention back to the music they'd been all but yelling over for the past hour or so. It was exactly what he would have expected of club music, though perhaps a touch more sassy than he was used to. It was also incredibly high energy and demanded the sort of dance Cade begrudgingly did with a good looking girl. The sort his mother would have sneeringly called 'bumping and grinding' or her favorite, 'sex with your clothes on' when she'd had a few drinks.

Elias eyed him, shrugging. "We *are* the guests of honor."

Cade wished he could shoot his friend a dirty look, but didn't dare with all the onlookers. Instead, he plastered a smile on his face and downed the last of his most recent drink. There wasn't exactly anything he could say, everyone, including both he and Elias, had been saying that the two of them were going to have to play along. And if that meant having to do a little bump and grind on the dancefloor, then well, he would suffer through it.

Thank God for alcohol.

As they stood up, Elias took Cade's hand in his own. For the first time, their hand to hand touch wasn't just a brief tap, or a squeeze before someone let go. Instead, Elias held on, holding onto Cade's hand firmly as he helped the man out of his seat and away from the others. Cade stared at their joined hands, a little amazed at just how small his hand looked in Elias', despite the fact that he'd never thought of his friend as all that much bigger than him. The realization sent a strange chill down Cade's arm, and he found himself a little distracted by the strength in Elias' grip before he realized his friend was speaking to him.

Cade looked up, wide-eyed. "What?"

Elias looked down at him, amusement creasing the corners of his eyes. "You uh, had that much to drink, huh?"

Jesus, had Elias always been this much bigger than him?

Cade scowled at him. "No, I was thinking. I think when I drink."

"About the only time you do."

"And here I thought you got mad at Matt for making that same joke earlier."

"Yeah, he's not me."

Cade smirked. "Only you can make fun of me for being an idiot, huh?"

"Yeah, because I'm the only one I trust to know you're not one."

Cade blinked. "Oh."

Elias shook his head. "And I'm going to be the first guy to dance with you and probably kiss you. Unless..."

Cade snorted. "No, I've never...wait, kiss?"

Elias rolled his eyes, and with a redoubled grip on Cade's wrist, pulled him toward the dance floor. Cade was still trying to process what the hell his friend was talking about before he realized he was standing amidst the crowd of people on the dance floor. Sight and sound merged, blending together in a kaleidoscope of sensation as he looked around, trying to get his bearings.

"'Kay, maybe I had a little bit," Cade muttered to himself, clinging to Elias.

"Can you dance?" Elias shouted, bending down so Cade could hear him.

Cade let out a laugh, shrugging. "Badly."

Elias smiled, reaching down, taking hold of Cade's hip and wrapping his other arm around his shoulders. "Good enough."

It was only as they began to move, with Cade following Elias' lead that he realized his friend could *move*. Even though the dance they were doing was the most cliché, grinding and humping thing he could think of, Elias' hips moved well. It didn't matter what direction Elias moved, his hips seemed to slide easily, smooth as silk and slick as oil, with a grace that left Cade wondering where the other man had been hiding it all along.

Then he was turned around, his heart thudding hard as he felt his back pressed to Elias' front. His friend's chest was strong, his stomach hard as he pressed against Cade, pushing against Cade's front as his hands roamed. Some part of him wanted to laugh, joke about the Latin blood that made Elias so smooth on the dancefloor, but the rest of his mind was distracted by Elias' motion, his grip on Cade's body, the sheer confidence with which he moved.

Watching, as if in a dream, Cade reached up and held tight to Elias, allowing himself to be guided. He wasn't even paying attention to the beat and rhythm of the music anymore. Both it and the sounds of the crowd were lost as his mind wrapped and warped around what was happening. It was...impressive, awesome in the truest sense of the word, as he felt his own body brought along for the ride and unable to stop itself from following the pace and moves that Elias set.

Then they were facing one another again, though it was done so smoothly, so quickly, that Cade was left blinking and wondering when they'd moved. Elias was gazing down at him, blue eyes glowing in the lights around them, and filled with an intensity that Cade had never seen before.

His heart leaped to his throat, breath clenching, and he knew what was coming. Cade could read it in Elias' eyes. Maybe if his logical brain was working, he might have told himself it was all for the show, all for the act. Yet all he knew was that Elias was going to kiss him. And that Cade wasn't going to stop him.

Their lips met, and Cade felt his breath catch in his throat at the absolute *hunger* of the kiss. His back arched, and he pushed against Elias, not to fight him, but to press closer, feel his rock hard body on every inch of his skin he could reach. His alcohol and hormone-filled mind swirled around in its thoughts, and he somehow found himself clutching to the back of Elias' head, holding tight and kissing him back just as fiercely.

And then it was over.

Elias pulled away, his brows stitched together as he slowly eased back. The man's grip fell away from Cade's body, gradually letting him take his own two feet again. Cade stood there, staring back at Elias as though paralyzed. His heart thumped hard, his lips tingling, and he was left with so many questions. Yet only one screamed in his mind, in both utter confusion and curiosity.

What the hell had just happened?

ELIAS

*W*hen he'd been younger, Elias had tried cocaine on a whim. He'd never wanted to touch anything as potentially mind warping as hallucinogens. Elias had never quite trusted anything that could make him see or feel things that didn't have a basis in reality. He'd been willing to try cocaine, though, despite how horrible some adults in his life had tried to make it out to be.

It ultimately hadn't been to his liking, but he still remembered the feeling. How it felt like his entire body had become a livewire. Sounds and colors had sharpened, becoming so much more interesting as his mind surged with processing power he'd never felt before. The room had felt as though it had come to life, beating with the pulse of life and energy unlike anything he'd ever known.

As he stood there, staring down at Cade after having just kissed him, Elias found his memories drifting back to that party. Just like then, his heart felt as though it were going a mile a minute. His lips were tingling, and he barely noticed that they were still standing in a jam-packed crowd.

Cade stared up at him dumbly, eyes wide, and his arms

slack at his side. Elias supposed the one comfort he could take from the storm in his head was that it looked like Cade wasn't faring much better. His friend's mouth was moving, though it was too noisy to tell if Cade was making a sound or just uselessly flapping his lips.

Before Elias was forced to find something to say, he realized there was a chorus of catcalls coming from behind them. Elias turned, facing the group that had come for the so-called celebration, watching them intently with grins on their faces. That was, except for Christine, who looked a lot like Cade in expression and manner, and Matt, who just stared at them with wide eyes.

Clearing his throat, he nodded his head back toward the group, earning him a jerky nod from Cade. Unsure if it was what he should be doing, he reached down to take hold of Cade's hand to lead him away from the dancefloor. Cade's fingers flexed against his hand but didn't pull away. The man's skin was hot, and Elias could feel a slick layer of sweat against his palm as they walked out of the crowd of still dancing people.

"Well, that was certainly something to see," Christine said when they reached the group.

Matt's brow was practically in his hairline as he spoke. "That was...something alright."

Elias shot him a look. "Yeah, I'm sure."

Matt slid two more glasses across the table. "Got these while you two were, uh, busy. Figured you might want some more."

Cade reached out and snatched up one of the glasses. "Thanks."

Elias' brow pinched, but he said nothing as he reached for the remaining glass. He wasn't sure what bothered him more, that Cade seemed extremely interested in getting even more drunk after what had happened, or that the thought bothered

Elias in the first place. Considering that was the first time they'd ever done anything that physically...intimate before, he should have been in the same boat.

Yet even the haze of alcohol wasn't enough to shake off the electric feeling of Cade's body against his. Sure, his friend wasn't exactly the world's most stellar dancer, but the dance had been...strangely erotic. Elias shook his head, not even listening to the conversation around him as he realized where his thoughts were going.

It had all been for show, a way to make Christine maybe ease back a bit, or at least calm her down for a little while. Hell, it was just supposed to be a dance. Yet as the two of them had ground and danced together, following only the rhythm of the music rather than any established pattern, Elias had found himself lost in it. The feel of Cade's body against his, the grip of his fingers on Elias' hips and shoulder.

And then he'd...kissed Cade.

An elbow pushed into his side, and Elias straightened. He blinked down at Cade, who was staring up at him with a raised eyebrow.

"Uh, what?" Elias asked dully, looking around.

Christine cocked her head, smirking. "I was just asking you where you learned to dance like that."

"And I said it was a good question," Cade added.

Elias thought Cade was remarkably composed for someone who had not only spent the entire past forty-eight hours fretting about the party but also for someone who, only minutes before, had looked he'd taken a good clubbing to the back of the head. Yet as Elias watched him, he could see the cool, casual, and friendly persona that Cade so often wore when he was out and about. Yet in the man's bright hazel eyes, Elias could see something else, a remnant of what had happened on the dancefloor, burning in the back of Cade's eyes.

"Ah, just a...natural talent, I guess?" Elias offered lamely.

Christine smiled. "A talent indeed. I'll admit, I rarely find myself...endeared to this sort of dancing. Club dancing."

Cade snorted. "Fucking with your clothes on."

To Elias' surprise, Christine's nose didn't wrinkle in distaste. Instead, her eyes widened in what he thought was a genuine expression of delight.

"Exactly," she answered.

Huh, maybe Elias didn't have her figured out quite as much as he'd thought.

Christine waved a hand through the air. "That said, I can almost understand why some people might enjoy it. And all because of you, Elias."

"Uh, me?" Elias asked.

Matt snorted softly to his left. "That's a really polite way of saying she appreciates the way you move your hips and take over."

Elias blinked. "Oh."

Christine looked at Matt. "I'm afraid I'm not familiar with you, but I must say, I'm growing to like you."

Matt eyed her, and with an expression of pure innocence, smiled. "I'm the original homosexual member of our station. I thought that's why you brought me to this little celebration of inclusivity and diversity."

Christine's face blanked. "I see."

"Oh shit," Cade snorted into his drink.

Even Elias broke out of his bewildered reverie to shoot Matt an appreciative smirk. Not once would he have thought that Matt had any sort of claws, subtle or otherwise, lurking beneath the surface. But as he watched Christine struggle to find the proper response to cover up her mistake, Elias had to appreciate the subtlety of Matt's work.

That was until a drunken Cade leaned against him, burying his face in Elias' arm as he tried to cover up his laughter. Elias sucked in a breath, stiffening as another electric jolt shot through him. Cade didn't seem to notice as he used his free hand to hold onto Elias and snigger quietly. Elias' heart thumped as he looked down at his friend, wondering what the hell was going on.

Cade looked up at him, and Elias' chest clenched as he realized that the same burning spark from before was still in his friend's eyes. It was buried under amusement and a haze of alcohol, but it was there all the same. The two of them stared at one another for what felt like forever. Eventually, Cade pulled away, his fingers the last to drift, almost reluctantly, from Elias' arm before facing Christine.

"Well, this gives you time to get acquainted with Matt," Cade said, eyes darting not to Matt, but Elias.

Christine brightened at the offered save. "Yes! Yes, of course. I'm so sorry I never noticed before. Perhaps you three...have some stories?"

Matt snorted, scooting aside to make room. "I'm sure we have a story or three waiting. C'mon you two drunk asses, sit next to me and be all couple like while we regale Christine with some stories."

"There are more than enough funny and good stories," Elias said, mostly as a subtle reminder that perhaps, considering what the night was about, bringing up the likes of Davis and Keith wasn't the best idea.

"Only the best," Matt promised.

Elias chuckled, sitting beside him and trying his best not to stiffen again as Cade scooted closer to sit down. A glance toward Cade told Elias that he wasn't the only one suddenly aware of their proximity. Yet the look of heat and wariness disappeared as Cade turned his attention to Christine across the table. He even barely flinched when Elias made a show, taking a breath before he did so, of placing his hand on Cade's thigh.

The feel of Cade's leg was warm, welcoming. And it terrified Elias almost as much as it interested him.

* * *

ELIAS HONESTLY WISHED he could say the night had grown easier. Instead, it seemed like the universe, and everyone at their party was intent on keeping Cade and Elias as close as possible. Elias was never given the chance to fully process what they'd done, what he'd done, when he and Cade had been on the dancefloor. All he knew was that the feel of Cade's body pushed against his, the brush of his fingers, sent another warm tingle through his body that drove straight to his groin.

What the hell was happening to him?

The answer didn't seem too interested in showing itself as the night continued. Not when he was forced to stand with his arm around Cade's waist, realizing how well Cade fit against him. His head always felt like it was swimming when Cade leaned against him, or when Cade lay a hand on him casually. It seemed like the more they drank, the more they forced themselves to play up the situation, the more Elias found himself constantly touching and holding onto Cade.

Elias almost let out a breath of relief when it came time for the club to close, and for all the patrons to be shooed out. That was until he stood on the sidewalk outside the club, with Cade leaning against him, and Matt smirking at them.

"What?" Elias asked.

"Nothing. I called you guys a cab," Matt told him.

"Oh. Thanks."

"Figured it would be easier than you guys going separately," Matt said with a glance toward Christine, who was chatting away with someone else.

"Mm, good point. Gotta be seen leaving with my hunky boyfriend, right?" Cade asked from beside him. His words were slurred around the edges, and there was obvious amusement in his voice.

"Hunky huh?" Matt asked.

"Very hunky. Big, tough, strong. Hunky."

"He's drunk," Elias said needlessly.

"And so are you. Just get home safe, guys. Text me in the morning," Matt said as the cab pulled up.

"You're so sweet, Matt. That's why I like you. You're just...so fucking nice. I'm sorry that Davis and Keith are assholes to you, you don't deserve that. Imma kick their asses the next time I see them," Cade promised as he worked his way carefully toward the cab.

"He's...drunk," Elias said, unable to help his smirk.

Matt patted his arm. "He's said something like that to me when he's sober too...just, with less slurring. So, not just drunk."

"No, he's..." Elias began

Matt shot him a look that Elias wasn't sure was understanding or commiseration. "He's Cade. Go on."

Cade leaned out of the cab. "Let's go, Elias. I wanna go cuddle."

"He's just saying that because she's right there?" Matt asked, glancing over his shoulder as he spoke in a whisper.

Elias chuckled, leaning in close. "No, he's actually pretty affectionate when no one else is around. He's just too drunk to realize he's announcing it to everyone right now."

Matt patted him. "Then get going before he starts professing his need for your hunky body or something."

Elias jerked. "I...what?"

Matt pushed him. "Go, before Christine tries to interfere."

That was all Elias needed to completely ignore anything weird and hop into the cab. Elias barked his address at the driver before closing the door and slumping in his seat. He only got a glimpse of Christine as she turned with a look of surprise on her face, watching the cab pass her by.

"Christ," Elias muttered, covering his face.

Warmth pressed against his side, and the familiar scent of Cade's cologne filled his nostrils. Elias had never bothered to find out what it was that Cade wore, but damned if he didn't recognize the scent immediately. It was somehow both spicy and earthy at the same time, and while he didn't know the exact scent, he realized it was one he immediately associated with Cade.

Cade leaned against his arm, sighing. "God, it's over."

Elias reached over, albeit a little hesitantly, and patted Cade's chest. "It is, buddy."

"Now we can go back to our place and just be us for a little bit. That'll be nice."

Elias hadn't missed the peculiar phrasing, though he said nothing. Since when had Cade started thinking of Elias' apartment as 'theirs'? Then again, did it really bother him all that much? Cade spent most of his leisure time at Elias' anyway, Elias wasn't even going to pretend to be surprised by his friend's attitude. Still, it was kind of nice to hear, much like the feel of him leaning against Elias for physical support was nice.

"Why're you so warm?" Cade muttered as he pressed closer to Elias.

"Latin blood," Elias teased.

"Mmm."

It was all Cade had to add to the conversation as he continued pressing against Elias. For his part, Elias was left with his own thoughts as the cab twisted and turned through the city streets taking them back to his apartment. His thoughts found themselves settling on the feel of Cade against him, how weirdly pleasurable it had felt to hold his friend close, and even more so, to kiss him. Elias had had no intention of kissing Cade, only to dance with him. But after the moment had gripped him, he'd found himself bending low and claiming Cade's lips for his own.

Elias shook his head slowly, trying to figure out where his thoughts were, or more specifically, what it was he was feeling. A twinge of what he couldn't help but realize was regret passed through him as they stopped outside his apartment complex, and he was forced to pull away from Cade. God save him, he was actually feeling drawn to the man and wanted to feel his touch.

"C'mon," Elias said, helping Cade out.

The brief nap seemed to have done the trick for Cade, however. He stepped out of the cab without a problem, though the same goofy, drunken smile was still on his face. Elias wasn't sure what the man was laughing at as they trudged up the stairs, but he said nothing as he let them into the apartment. He did, however, raise a brow as he watched Cade disappear into the kitchen and reappear with two open beers.

"Haven't had enough?" Elias asked.

"Oh c'mon, it's just a couple of beers. In the sea of booze we've drunk tonight, what's two beers while you and I just...be?"

He couldn't argue with the logic, and he took the beer from the other man. Their fingers brushed against one another, and he'd swear Cade's eyes flashed to his face with that same burning look from before. Rather than think about it too much, Elias marched into the living room and plopped down onto the couch. Cade was right behind him, mindlessly humming a tune as he followed suit, sitting on the middle cushion, right next to Elias.

"Think she's happy?" Cade asked as he took a deep drink from the bottle.

"Who, Christine?"

"Yeah."

Elias shrugged. "I don't know. For the moment."

Cade took another deep drink and belched. "Well, fuck her. I actually had fun."

"Did you now?" Elias asked in amusement, thinking of how nervous and fretful Cade had been at the start of the evening.

Cade set the beer down on the coffee table with a hard thump, nodding. "Damn right, I did."

"I'm sure the alcohol helped."

Cade sagged, laying himself across the couch until his head was in Elias' lap. Elias stiffened as Cade's head lay against his legs, Cade's hand gripping his thigh. His heart began to thud as his mind raced back to the feeling of Cade's body against him, the pure electric pleasure of the kiss they'd shared.

"Alcohol was good. But I had fun," Cade said, wriggling into a more comfortable position.

Jesus, was he getting hard?

Yessir, his pants were starting to feel constricting.

"I'm...glad you enjoyed yourself," Elias said through a tight throat.

Cade nodded. "I did. Thank you."

"Why are you thanking me?" Elias asked, taking a drink.

"Because you were there. You were with me. You helped."

"Don't really think I did all that much."

Cade patted his thigh. "Don't be like that. You were a lot of help."

God, the tightness in his pants was becoming painful.

"Well, fine. I'm glad I could help," Elias said.

Cade made a happy humming noise, his fingers stroking the inside of Elias' thigh. Elias stared down at his friend, watching as his fingers grew closer and closer. The outline of

Elias' cock was spreading down his pants, and the thought that Cade might just reach it with his fingers made it grow even more. As he'd predicted, Cade's fingers brushed over the hard length a few times, drawing a low breath from Elias.

Cade's movements stopped. A frown creased his brow, and his fingers stroked the area of Elias' thigh again. Elias' sucked in a breath, knowing he should tell Cade to stop, that…that was his dick. But instead, he watched, waiting as Cade's fingers slowly, carefully, but inevitably traced the outline of Elias' cock.

"Oh," Cade whispered.

"Yeah," Elias said, voice shaking.

Cade's fingers didn't leave, though. They didn't move, but they stayed where they were, resting against the now completely hard outline of Elias' cock.

"I guess," Cade began.

Elias raised his brow, wondering what was coming next from his friend's mouth. Before he had to reply, however, Cade's fingers closed around Elias' cock, squeezing it tentatively. A low groan escaped Elias' lips before he could think of what he was doing, and he felt Cade's body stiffen against him.

"Oh," Cade muttered.

Elias, through half-lidded eyes, looked over Cade's body and remembered what it felt like to have it against him. His eyes felt drawn to his friend's groin, breath catching as he caught sight of a bulge that hadn't been there before. Feeling like he was back in the dream state of the dance floor, Elias reached out, cupping Cade's crotch. Cade's breath was sharp, but he didn't pull away as Elias' fingers curled around his cock.

God, Cade was hard.

He was hard.

They were enjoying this.

Not knowing or caring if it was the alcohol in their system, Elias grasped the button of Cade's jeans and pulled it. Next came the zipper, the sound filling the air among their heavy breathing. Cade's hands never moved away from his groin, only his grip around Elias' cock tightening as Elias' hand slipped beneath the band of Cade's underwear.

And there it was.

His fingers brushed along the steel-hard length of Cade's cock. It was the first cock other than his own that Elias had ever touched. Instead of the expected repulsion, Elias felt a surge of excitement as he wrapped his hand around the shaft and pulled Cade's cock free.

"Oh, God," Cade muttered, pushing into Elias' touch.

It was then that Elias felt his own pants loosen, and Cade's hand rooting roughly inside. Elias gave a choked gasp as Cade's rough hand wrapped around his cock, pulling him free and letting out a moan as the pressure was released.

"Jesus, Eli," Cade said.

"Sorry."

"No wonder the ladies like you."

Elias couldn't help his laugh. His dick wasn't huge, but it was certainly in proportion to the rest of him. Yet for the first time, he wasn't bathing in the attention of a woman over his dick, but that of a man, and not just any man. God, it was Cade with his fingers wrapped around Elias' cock, holding it tightly, looking at it in awe. And in turn, he had Cade's cock in his own grip.

God, what were they doing?

Yet the moment he moved his hand, jerking Cade slowly, he got his answer. Cade's low moan, and the shudder that pulled through him, was enough to wipe all worry and concern from Elias' throat.

In turn, Cade's hand stroked his own cock, and between the sensation and the knowledge that it was Cade attached to him, Elias let out a deep groan. It seemed like neither one of them was thinking too hard about what they were doing. Instead, Cade pushed himself upright, so he was sat next to Elias, careful not to break their hold on one another.

"Oh shit," Elias moaned, leaning forward and claiming Cade's lips with his own again.

Again he hadn't planned on it, but again, he felt the electric surge of pleasure rip through him.

"Elias," Cade moaned, thrusting against Elias' touch.

Elias felt Cade's cock throb against his palm, and he knew what was happening. His own body responded, pleasure ramping up as Cade's grip tightened. Warmth spread over his fingers as Cade came with a low groan, pressing closer to him. Elias was not far behind, letting out a deep noise as he came over his shirt and Cade's grip. For one moment, they shared their pleasure, their ecstasy, shared it in a way neither of them had ever done before. Shared it in a way Elias had never dreamed of ever doing.

Yet…

"Elias," Cade gasped, his pupils swelling.

Elias stared at him, his mind seizing up just as his body had only moments before. Shaking his head, he smiled.

"Sleep," Elias told him.

"But," Cade began, looking down at their cum covered hands, their cocks now wilting since the moment had passed.

"Tomorrow," Elias said, even as his mind screamed for answers.

God, he'd wanted it, just as much as Cade had. But they were…they weren't like that. Especially not with one another. Yet they had. They'd done it.

"I don't know," Cade began.

And Elias spoke the truth he knew deep in himself. Knowing that no matter how much their own stuporous minds might try to scream otherwise.

"Booze will get us nice and sleepy," Elias told him.

And maybe it would bring the oblivion of forgetfulness. Maybe they could forget this ever happened, that the whole damn night even happened. Above all else, maybe Elias could forget the feeling of his best friend's cock in his hand, while Cade's was wrapped around his own. Maybe he could forget the intoxicating feel of Cade's mouth against his, and the sheer pleasure of hearing Cade call out his name.

"Sleep," Elias said, helping him up to get them to bed.

But the question was, did he really want to forget?

CADE

*W*ith a low, pained groan, Cade rose to consciousness. It was a slow, uncomfortable process, not at all helped by the realization of what he knew was a hangover. As his mind sluggishly roused itself, he became aware of an ache in his neck, radiating down to his back and up into his skull. He'd apparently laid in one spot for too long, and it felt like the entire upper portion of his back had seized up.

With another dull noise, he rolled over, wincing as the sunlight from the bedroom window spilled over his face. This time, he let out a soft whimper, burying his face in the pillow to escape the wretched sunlight. He'd known the night before that he was going to wake up miserable as hell, but being prepared didn't make his suffering any less.

Yet, his bladder was not going to let him stay in bed for much longer.

"Yeah, yeah, I hear ya," he grumbled at his body.

Pushing himself up with excruciating slowness, he winced against the sunlight once again. Thankfully, it didn't seem like his headache was too bad. A big glass of water, along with some medicine, would have that gone within the hour. Yet that wouldn't be enough to shake off the utterly gross feeling running through him. And that included his mouth. He swore he didn't remember licking any garbage last night, but it sure tasted like he had.

Stumbling gracelessly to Elias' bathroom, he made his way to the toilet. As he finally gave his bladder what it wanted, he couldn't help but be glad he hadn't ended up praying to the porcelain god at any point. The few times he'd been stupid enough to let himself drink so heavily he'd thrown up had resulted in the worst hangovers of his life. This one was a pretty bad one, but it's one he could live with. Hell, if he had to, he could even work through it, so long as he didn't have to do too much.

Good thing he didn't have to work.

It was Sunday, and he was free to spend the remainder of his day off to himself, without having to go into work. That was probably exactly why the chief had decided to give him the day off on Sunday as well. No doubt, the older man had known what kind of state Cade would have been in if he'd been forced to come to the station. While Cade would have preferred to actually enjoy his day off, it beat trying to nurse a hangover at work.

Washing his hands, he shuffled out into the hallway with a low groan, and into the kitchen. The first thing he did was grab a bottle of water, and snatch the pill bottle off the counter. Elias must have set it there before leaving for the club, knowing he and Cade would end up back at his place. Cade popped a few into his mouth and downed the entire bottle of water in a series of heavy gulps. With that out of the way, he went about making a big pot of coffee. The only times he ever wanted coffee was when he was meeting someone for a fancy, sugar and fat-laden cup of it at a cafe, or when he was hungover and just needed the caffeine boost.

His neck twinged as he poured the water into the reservoir, and he silently cursed Christine. If it hadn't been for her petty need to play some stupid game, he wouldn't be standing in Elias' kitchen in his boxers, hungover and sore. He'd been thrust in front of a bunch of people, half of which were perfect strangers, and made to dance. It had been humiliating, stressful, and he hoped he never had to repeat the process ever again.

Well, at least Elias had been by his side. His friend had come through for him, just as he knew he would. Cade smiled faintly as he hit the brew button on the machine. Elias had put up with a lot the night before, and it hadn't even been his fault he and Cade were in that mess. But Elias had stood by him, escorting him, playing the part, even dancing with him. Cade paused, remembering the kiss, and remembering...

Cade's eyes widened, spinning around to stare in the direction of the living room. He'd turned too quickly though and had to grip onto the counter before the dizziness forced him to fall over. Cade barely noticed his near fall, however, his mind firmly on the previous night's conclusion.

Shit, how had he almost forgotten?

The kiss had been one thing. Sure, it had been shocking, and Cade would have never believed that Elias would have kissed him, let alone that Cade would have, well maybe not liked it, but not...or maybe he had. But even then, he could brush that off, and he thought he had. Yes, the kiss had lingered, as had the memory of how easily, confidently, Elias had taken over the dance, moving so fluidly, and even kissed him without the slightest trace of hesitancy or doubt. But it had been a strange night, with weird circumstances, surely odd things were bound to crop up.

But then he'd laid there, his head in Elias' lap, and he'd...felt the man's cock. They'd seen each other naked before, but Cade had never seen, let alone felt Elias' hard cock. In his drunken haze, he'd been a little amazed by it. He could remember thinking that Elias definitely didn't have anything to be ashamed of. It was no monster, but it was bound to be eye-catching.

And he'd kept touching it.

Cade's breath caught, and his fingers gripped the edge of the counter fiercely. Elias had touched him too, and the next thing he knew, both of their cocks were out and in one another's hands. Neither of them stopped to think about what they were doing, or if they were even supposed to be doing it. Cade had just felt the strong, calloused hands of Elias wrapped around his cock, and all he could think was how much he didn't want it to stop.

The smell of coffee began to fill the kitchen, turning his stomach. He clenched his eyes shut, shaking his head in a dull attempt to fight off the rising wave of nausea. He'd had a guy get him off, and not just any guy, but his best friend, his *straight* best friend.

God, could he even use that word to describe them anymore?

Still refusing to let his stomach flip so hard that he got sick, Cade turned around and walked to the sink. Turning the cold water on full blast, he reached in, cupping it to splash against his face. The frigid water was a welcome contrast to his warm skin, jolting him enough that his stomach stopped feeling like it was at sea during a storm. He continued to splash water against his face as the images of Elias' cock, the man's hand around Cade's cock, and the sound of Elias' deep groan as he…

Cade shook his head again. No, this was not happening, he was not going to do this. He was not going to let his mind fall down the rabbit hole of last night. His life was already weird enough, with his mother breathing down his neck,

Christine prepared to hound him every chance she got, and everyone unwittingly playing along with her little game.

"God, Christine, what the fuck," Cade muttered, turning the cold water off with a shove of his arm.

What had they done?

He was no closer to an answer, or even being remotely calm when he heard movement from down the hallway. Cade's head jerked up, fingers tightening around the edge of the sink as he strained his ears. The sounds weren't coming any closer, and after a moment, he heard the bathroom door click closed quietly. Cade continued to stand at the sink, heart racing furiously, as he heard the toilet flush. A soft breath of momentary relief left him as the shower turned on.

Maybe it wasn't the noblest thing, but he knew what he had to do.

Knowing that Elias would probably stand under the hot water of the shower, hoping to evaporate his own hangover, Cade hurried down to the bedroom. Careful not to thump around, he snatched up his phone and ordered a ride to the apartment. Pulling on his pants and shirt, he searched around for his socks. A thud from the bathroom brought his head up again, and he listened, only when it was followed by softer thumps did Cade allow himself to relax and resume his search.

He had to give up on his socks when his phone beeped at him, alerting him that his ride was there. Shoving his bare feet into his shoes, he gathered up his phone and keys. With another glance toward the bathroom, he hurried as quietly as he could to the front door. He made sure to lock the door behind him, and finally fled down the stairs and out the front door of the apartment complex. His ride was waiting for him at the front curb, and Cade threw himself into it and rattled off the address.

It was only when they were out of the complex and on

the road that Cade allowed himself to take a deep breath. He couldn't face Elias, not right now, not when his thoughts felt thick and heavy, swirling around like molasses being forced down a greedy drain. He couldn't...deal with what happened, not right now. He would message Elias, tell him he was going to go suffer through his hangover in solitude, and he'd see him tomorrow.

God, he just needed to think, just for a few hours.

* * *

IT TURNED out that a few hours was not enough to make him feel better. Sure, his hangover was dwindling. All it had taken was a quick hot shower at his own place and a vast quantity of hot food, and he was physically feeling better as the hours ticked by. Another dose of pain relievers later and the kink in his neck and back had even eased.

None of that did anything to ease his nerves, however.

Cade rubbed at his face, groaning. He'd tried to zone out on something, but nothing could hold his attention. Watching a movie resulted in him losing track of the movie's plot within ten minutes of turning it on. Trying to read had been an equal failure, with Cade having to reread the same paragraph half a dozen times before he realized he still wasn't understanding what was on the page.

It honestly didn't matter what he did, he couldn't keep his mind off what had happened. Cade had managed to determine that if it had been anyone else, he might have been able to deal with it. Hell, sometimes a guy got drunk and did something that was completely out of character, and just born of both the moment and the drinks pounding through his system.

But it hadn't been just any guy.

And as much as he wanted to blame the alcohol, he really

couldn't. Sure, they had both been pretty damn drunk, but he'd been drunker before, and so had Elias. Yet in all the times before they'd got shit faced drunk with one another, they'd never groped one another. Hell, they'd slept in the same bed several times before and never did so much as cuddle.

They weren't afraid to be close, physically, and away from prying eyes. Being around Elias was warm and comforting to Cade. Elias was honestly the first person Cade had ever met who he felt like he could just...be. There was no need for pretense, Cade didn't have to act a certain way or present a front to make Elias happy. And while he'd never outright admitted it, he liked touching Elias and being touched by him. A hand on the shoulder, or when Cade would read and lean against Elias. There was a sturdiness to the man, a quiet strength that seemed to ooze out of his pores. Cade wasn't ashamed to, privately, admit that he loved those moments.

But how the hell did that translate into a full-blown drunken moment of mutual masturbation?

For what felt like the hundredth time, he picked up his phone and stared at his messages with Elias. Just as he'd promised himself, he'd messaged the man and told him what his plan was. There was no way Elias didn't know why Cade had mysteriously disappeared. Cade wasn't one to just leave without warning, and he knew if he remembered what happened the night before, then Elias most certainly had.

Yet Elias had said nothing in his return text, telling Cade to remember to drink plenty of water and text if he needed anything. Cade had found himself continually coming back to the message, wondering if he should say anything. The problem was, he had no idea what the hell he was supposed to even say.

"Hey, remember when we jerked each other off last night?" Cade said aloud, giving an ugly snort.

Yeah, right, that was just what he was going to do.

Cade shook his head and shoved his phone in between the couch cushions. There was no way in hell he was going to bring it up. And from the looks of it, neither was Elias. Maybe that was precisely what they needed to do, just let the sleeping dragon lie and not bother with disturbing its little nap.

It wasn't like they didn't already have enough on their plates. They didn't need to add something that was just...so outside of the realm of normal to the mix as well. Sure, it had happened, but that didn't mean they had to give it any more attention than was necessary.

No need to go into detail about how Elias had kissed him again, and that Cade suspected he might have liked it at that moment. Unnecessary to go over how right Elias' hand had felt wrapped around his dick, or how he'd found his mind drifting to a few other things they might be able to do if they were feeling bold enough.

And there was definitely no need to mention that the memories were enough to make his stomach tighten, and for his cock to give an interested twitch.

"No more, no more," Cade repeated, closing his eyes and forcing a deep breath.

He managed two whole breaths before his phone started ringing. Cade jerked, fumbling beside him to pull out the phone, his heart in his throat. His heart sank when he stared at the number on the caller ID.

"Aw hell," he muttered, just what he needed.

Gritting his teeth, he answered. "Hey, Mom."

Pamela huffed through the receiver. "Do not 'hey' me, Kaidan. You're a full-grown man with a good education, use your words properly."

Cade stared up at the ceiling. "Hello, Mother."

"Better. Now I was hoping to get your opinion on the celebration at the end of the month."

Cade stiffened. "Celebration?"

"Yes, Kaidan, dear. The City Council is holding a charity celebration for, what was it again? Oh yes, because crime and damage from fires have been going down for a few years now."

"Oh right, that."

"Yes, that. And you know full well *everyone* of any importance is going to be there. So I was thinking about what you might wear."

Cade rolled his eyes, settling into the couch and prepared for a normal conversation with his mother. "Were you now?"

"Yes."

And without prompting, she immediately launched into her ideas. Cade listened long enough to realize he would probably have to go in for another fitting before it was all said and done. After that, he began to lose track of his mother's words, zoning out as his mother droned on.

It might not have been the solution he was looking for, but at least his mother was a good distraction.

ELIAS

*E*lias rubbed at his face, trying to jostle himself awake. His eyes drifted up to the clock on the mess hall's wall and frowned at it. There was no way it was only one in the afternoon. It felt like he'd been at the station for a double shift, not half of one.

"That can't be right," Elias muttered to himself.

Things had a tendency to break down around the station, but the clock had always been reliable. Even Cade had sworn up and down that the thing was more accurate than any cellphone was, though Elias had never sought to test it. But considering how he felt, maybe he should ask the chief if they should look at it and make sure.

His thoughts were interrupted as a steaming cup of coffee was plopped down in front of him. Elias looked up, blinking, and couldn't help the sinking in his stomach when he saw Matt standing there with a smirk on his face. Cade was in the station, but he'd been incredibly careful to avoid being around Elias for too long. They had, of course, greeted one another that morning, just as they had the day before, and the day before that. Elias had expected the awkwardness

118

on Monday and had even tolerated it on Tuesday. Now it was Wednesday, and Elias found himself beginning to wonder if they were ever going to look one another in the eye again for more than five seconds, let alone have a conversation.

"You looked like you were about to pass out," Matt offered as he sat across from Elias.

"Thanks," Elias muttered, picking the cup up.

The station coffee had been one of the few changes Elias himself had enforced. When he'd first arrived over two years before, the coffee had been the equivalent of dirt with a hint of bitterness. When the chief refused to upgrade to anything else, Elias had started buying his own huge tub of grounds and let the others help themselves. Eventually, it had gotten to the point that everyone started buying the next tub, rotating through whose turn it was. Even the chief had begrudgingly got in on the act, and the nasty stuff had sat in the cabinets, rotting away for all Elias cared.

Elias raised a brow as it hit his tongue. "Oof, Davis didn't make this."

Matt laughed. "Nope, that was me."

"I forget you like it strong," Elias said.

"Damn right I do," Matt said with a wicked grin.

Elias snorted. "Not what I meant."

"No, but I'll take it."

"I'm sure you will."

Matt snorted. "Touché."

Just in time to dissolve the hint of a good mood Elias might have been forming, Cade walked in. His eyes darted nervously to Elias' face and then shot over to Matt. What might have been an attempt at a smile, but looked more like a grimace, crossed his face as he raised a hand.

"Well, howdy Cade, kind of forgot you were here," Matt said, leaning back in his seat.

"Chief had me doing inventory. I guess no one's done it for a while," Cade said, moving over to the coffee machine.

Elias snorted softly. Right, because Cade hadn't been finding different things to do around the station that kept him away from the rest of them for the past three days or anything. He had no doubt the chief had told Cade to do it, but he also suspected that Cade had been the one to inform the chief of the lack of recent inventory taking too.

"Careful," Matt warned. "I made the coffee."

"Can't be any worse than when Elias makes it," Cade said as he poured himself a cup.

"Thanks, buddy," Elias said.

Cade turned with a steaming cup in hand. "Everyone knows you don't make coffee, you make sludge."

"Tastes fine to me."

Cade shrugged. "I guess you're just used to it."

Matt eyed him. "And apparently, so are you. But uh, since when do you drink coffee?"

Cade gave another shrug. "Haven't been sleeping."

His eyes darted again to Elias and held there for a moment. Elias had undoubtedly noticed the more pronounced bags under his eyes lately. They were probably just as dark the ones on his own face.

Matt snorted. "After how much you two put away Saturday night, I wouldn't be surprised if you were still hungover."

"I'm not hungover," Cade muttered, averting his eyes from Elias.

Neither of them was hungover, but Elias still felt ill all the same.

"We've done worse," Elias said.

"Yeah," Cade agreed.

"Haven't got you two in the same room while I've been

around since the party. You guys have a good night?" Matt asked.

Unsurprisingly, Elias watched Cade tense up as he nodded. "Yeah, it was actually uh, a good time. Surprising."

"I think Christine was pretty surprised too," Matt said.

"I'm sure she was," Cade muttered. "Anyway, I'm going to get back to it. There's still more inventory to do."

"I thought you said you were done?" Elias asked.

"Did I? My bad," Cade called as he marched out of the room.

Matt stared at the doorway, a single brow raising. "Okay, what's up with him?"

Elias stared down at his drink. "Well, I guess you'll have to take that up with him."

Matt's head jerked back toward him. "Okay, what's up with you?"

"I haven't been sleeping."

"Yeah, I noticed that. I also noticed he hasn't been sleeping either."

"People have a hard time sleeping sometimes, Matt, it happens."

But was he having a hard time sleeping because of what had happened Saturday night? Because Cade was barely able to exist around Elias without wanting to skitter out of the room as quickly as possible? Or was it just because he missed having his friend over, having someone who eased his mind so he could sleep through the night?

Matt snorted, setting his cup down. "Really? You're going to pull the brick wall act on me now?"

"What?"

"That thing you do where you pretend like everything is fine and any attempt to get you to talk about it is met with the emotional equivalent of running face-first into a brick wall."

Elias stared at him. It wasn't the first time someone had complained about his stubbornness to talk, but it was the first time someone had ever put it so eloquently. It wasn't going to make him talk any more freely, either.

Keith's voice echoed down the hall. "And I told her it wasn't going to work, but she didn't listen. Now I've got a cleaning bill that's almost as much as my fucking rent."

"Why didn't you stop her?" Davis asked as the two of them entered the mess hall.

"Because I didn't think it would be *that* big of a mess," Keith told him.

"You were wrong."

Keith stopped before replying, spotting Matt and Elias at one of the tables. Elias stared back, not giving a shit if the man's face blanked and irritation curled at his lip. Of all the things on the list of problems he had in his life that needed to be dealt with, Keith's stupidity didn't even make the bottom ten.

"Afternoon," Matt called to them cheerfully.

Keith grunted, jerking his head with what might have been a greeting, and made his way over to the coffee machine. Keith had never been the most friendly of guys, not to anyone but Davis that was, but he'd been even more grumpy ever since the news about Elias and Cade's 'relationship' had been announced.

"What're you two doing in here?" Davis asked as he waited his turn for the machine.

Matt raised a cup. "Same thing you're doing."

Keith glanced back with a snort. "Your boyfriends know you're in here all cozy with one another?"

Elias bridled, but Matt beat him to it, replying with a smile. "Cade was just in here and talked with us for a bit. And yeah, my boyfriend knows I work in a station with a bunch of other guys."

"Guys like you?" Keith asked with a smirk.

"He's aware, yeah," Matt told him.

Keith gave another snort, stepping out of the way to let Davis get at the machine. "And yours?"

Elias knew the question was directed at him but had to bite down on his tongue. His first knee jerk reaction was to tell Keith to stop referring to him and Cade as boyfriends. Yet that instinctive comment flew in the face of the charade that he and Cade were carrying on.

Elias didn't look up from his cup. "You heard Matt."

Keith looked him over. "You seem grumpy. You and your boyfriend having a lover's spat?"

"Keith," Davis muttered from behind him.

Elias looked up slowly, feeling a muscle in his jaw twitch. "You know his name. Use it."

"Doesn't answer my question."

"And it's none of your business."

"Shit, you guys were good enough to share your business with everyone before, but now it's a big secret?"

Elias watched him come closer, forcing himself to keep calm. Suddenly his thought that Keith wasn't much of a problem seemed less and less true as he was forced to deal with him. Three days of little to no sleep weren't helping, and he could feel his nerves tightening way too quickly, way too tightly.

"Not a secret. Just none of your business," Elias said, forcing his voice to stay calm.

"Or maybe you're just not wanting to admit that you aren't into this shit at all. Maybe you two just had yourselves a little bit of fun and realized pussy is where you really wanna be. So now you're having yourselves a little fight...or is it that one of you liked it more than the other."

Elias' head snapped up. "Shut your fucking mouth, Keith."

Keith gave a derisive laugh. "Touchy."

Elias pushed out of his seat, smacking Keith's cup out of his hand. The man gave a yelp as the hot coffee splashed over him. Elias reached out, grabbing Keith by his shirt front and yanking him close. Nearly face to face, the size difference between the two of them couldn't have been more apparent. Keith still had to look up with wide eyes into Elias' face, and he still had at least another thirty, maybe forty pounds before he'd weigh as much.

"Holy shit, Elias!" Davis yelped, dropping his cup.

Matt leaned back, mouth dropping open but said nothing.

Elias leaned in until his nose almost touched Keith's. He'd always been conscious of his size ever since he'd started growing as a teen. His size and strength had made him a target for a lot of other idiots who'd wanted to prove themselves against a big opponent. Elias had defended himself more times than he would have liked to, and it had left him with the awareness of just how terrifying he could be. It was something he never wanted, but by God, he was going to use it now.

"Shut your *fucking mouth*, or I'll do it for you," Elias growled.

"Elias," Matt began.

Elias didn't pull his eyes away from Keith. "No, I'm sick of this shit. Just because you think being with a dude is gross doesn't mean you get to run your mouth. I've been listening to you for two years, Keith, and I'm over it. I'm tired, I don't feel good, and I'm sick of your shit. The next time I hear you say anything nasty, to me, to Cade, to Matt, I'm laying you out? You hear me?"

Keith fought to keep his features in a snarl. "Fuck you."

Elias released him. "Then try me, big boy, just try me."

Keith stumbled back from the table, his chin dripping coffee still. His dark eyes blazed with fury and wounded pride. Elias stood there, letting Keith be stupid enough to make the first move or to open his mouth. Instead, the seconds ticked by, before Keith finally gave a low snarl, turning on one heel and walking away.

"Jesus," Davis muttered.

"The same goes for you," Elias told him.

Davis held up his hands. "Heard. Understood."

Grunting, Elias sat down back in his seat, pulling his coffee toward him once again. He wasn't sure how the cup hadn't been knocked over in the scuffle, but he was just glad he didn't have to get up for another cup. Elias took his time taking his next sip, ignoring the glance Matt and Davis shared before Davis finally took off after his friend.

Matt eased back in his seat, watching Elias. "So…"

Elias sighed. "What?"

"You sure you don't want to tell me what's going on between you and Cade?"

"What makes you think he has anything to do with it?"

"You know being gay doesn't mean I'm blind, right? Just means I like dudes."

Elias scowled at him. "I never said anything like that."

"Right, because you two haven't been weird around one another since you came back on Monday. You haven't been sleeping, which while not weird, it's normally not this bad. Cade's not sleeping, and he normally sleeps like a damn baby. And I've never seen you lose your temper before, so how about we just save the bullshit, and you tell me what's going on. Is the whole fake relationship thing getting to you guys?" Matt asked softly, making sure his voice didn't carry.

Elias closed his eyes, didn't he wish?

Shaking his head, Elias muttered. "No. Something…happened on Saturday."

"Something?" Matt asked with a raised brow.

Elias shifted uncomfortably in his chair, staring resolutely at his cup. "We were on the couch, drinking a beer and talking. And…"

Matt leaned forward, eyes widening after he read Elias' face. "You…you guys…did you sleep together?"

Elias winced, feeling his face warm. "No, but we did something."

"Something?"

Unable to make the words come out, Elias made a jerk-off motion.

"Side by side, or like, did it *to* one another."

Elias looked up with a frown, not caring that his cheeks were probably red. "Do you want the intimate details? Wanna know what our dicks look like?"

Matt covered his mouth, snickering. "I'm sorry. I'm just…a little, okay a lot shocked actually. I mean, I knew you guys were faking it, but I always assumed there was nothing…there, you know?"

"I know. Neither did I. And neither did Cade."

"Huh, I thought something was up that night."

"What do you mean?"

"I saw you two dancing, and I saw that kiss. If I hadn't known you guys were supposed to be acting, I would have said…"

"What?"

Matt took a deep breath. "I would have said you two looked like a pair of guys either on your way or well into falling in love with one another."

Oh.

"But I just told myself it was a good act, and after all, you two *are* pretty close."

Elias snorted softly. "Were."

Matt rolled his eyes. "Don't be dramatic."

"Uh, excuse me?"

"You two ran into the first thing in your two years of

friendship that has made it hard to talk to one another. Sometimes it's a fight, sometimes it's uh, jerking each other off."

"Thanks for being so tactful."

"My point is, don't let this one thing be the thing that ruins the friendship. Don't sit around and be awkward for weeks, not when he's right there. You're both obviously struggling with this, don't let it go on for too long."

Elias wasn't so sure it was that simple. While he did feel a little better talking to Matt about it, it still didn't leave out the squirming uneasiness in his gut. The weirdest part of it all wasn't that he regretted it, though he certainly was regretting the results of it. He probably should have been a little more worried, considering this was both his best friend he'd fucked around with, but also another guy.

"I don't know if it...I don't want shit to be weird," Elias said.

Matt raised a brow. "What were you going to say first?"

Elias looked down at his cup, shaking his head. "Nothing."

"You were going to say something about liking it, weren't you?"

"You're not going to let me keep anything to myself, are you?"

Matt grinned. "It's okay to like it. And it's okay if you want to do it again, and more."

Elias said nothing, not wanting to admit the thoughts had been in his head.

"But that's not what's bothering you, is it?" Matt asked quietly.

Elias sighed. "No. I can...I can deal okay with the idea that it happened, and that it was...fun. I can deal with the idea that it made me a little more curious than before."

"I'd say I'm surprised since most straight guys would take

it as an earth-shattering blow that they did something with another dude and liked it."

Elias shrugged. "It's weird, yeah. Never thought about it before, and never wanted it before. But I mean, it's Cade."

Matt snorted. "Of course, that's your answer."

"What's that supposed to mean?" Elias asked indignantly.

Matt reached over, squeezing Elias' hand. "It means you two have always been really close, like close enough that I'm not surprised people made comments about you two supposedly dating. Close enough that I'm not surprised you're okay with what happened because it's him."

"But Cade," Elias began, trailing off.

Matt squeezed his hand once more. "Well, there's your hurdle. You're going to have to talk to him. Sooner would be better than later. Find out where his head is at."

"Probably nowhere good."

Matt pushed away from the table, draining the last of his coffee. "Look, I have to go scrub out the oil stains on the front drive and sidewalk, or chief will have my ass. But you have to be willing to sit down with him and talk. Figure out what he thinks, what he feels. You guys are never going to get past this...whatever it is, without talking it out."

"Yeah, I guess," Elias said.

Matt chuckled, throwing his cup away. "Both of you are being stubborn and weird. Which is fine. Just don't let it go on so long that you're both being stupid about it instead."

Elias fiddled with his cup in the silence.

"Till Friday, I'll give him that long," Elias told himself.

Hopefully, he didn't drop from exhaustion before then.

CADE

$\mathcal{C}$ade had experienced long weeks before, but none as long as the one where he and Elias had been practically strangers to one another. The worst part was, he knew it was his own damn fault. He was the one who was choosing to stay away from Elias, and his friend was simply respecting Cade's unspoken wish to be left alone. Cade knew he had to suck it up at some point and talk to Elias, but the problem was, he didn't know what he was supposed to say.

Hey, I know we had a bit of hand on dick fun, but that's left me feeling like my head is imploding?

Cade shook the thought away, irritated that despite having spent days thinking, he still hadn't come up with anything better. There wasn't exactly a handbook for what to do when you somehow found yourself getting sexually active with your straight best friend while you too, were straight. And the one person he would have talked to about it was Elias, so that wasn't going to help.

He lay his head against the truck he was scrubbing out, and let out a sigh.

"You alright?"

Elias' voice brought Cade upright with a startled grunt. Spinning around, he spotted Elias standing at the door to the hallway, concern etched into his face.

"Yeah, just, tired of scrubbing every last corner of this thing," Cade grumbled, turning back toward the truck.

Which was true. The chief expected that every time the truck went out, it had to be cleaned, and deep cleaned at that. Which meant every nook and cranny, every corner of every compartment, had to be wiped and cleaned. Since Matt had gone out for his little demonstration at the school earlier that day, that meant the truck had to be cleaned.

"Matt said you offered to do it," Elias said.

Cade grimaced. "Yep, and I'm regretting it as we speak."

"You know he'd come out and help if you asked."

"Yeah, but I'm not asking."

"Stubborn."

"That's me."

Silence hung around them again, and Cade felt the oppressive tension begin to sink in. Cade didn't turn around though, he didn't want to see the dark bags under Elias' eyes. He didn't want to know that Elias, who already had sleep problems as it was, was sleeping even worse than usual. God, he felt bad enough about the whole thing, he didn't want to add even more guilt on top of things.

Elias cleared his throat. "Look, Cade…"

Cade closed his eyes again, his movement against the truck's exterior stopping. Was Elias really going to do this here?

"I really think it's about time we talk," Elias continued.

"Yeah?" Cade asked.

"Yeah, as a matter of fact, I know it's time."

Cade couldn't help his small smile. He would bet Elias had set a quiet little deadline in his head of when he was going to say something. Plenty of people would have done the same thing in his place, but Cade knew that when Elias made up his mind, it was made. Elias could call Cade stubborn all he wanted, but Cade had yet to meet someone as bullheaded and determined as Elias when he'd made a decision.

Cade finally forced himself to turn around and face his exhausted friend. "I really don't think right now is a good time."

In the firehouse? Yeah, that would be great. All they would need would be for the chief or Keith to come wandering out and hear them talking about the awkwardness of Saturday night. Then not only would everyone know the whole he and Elias thing dating was a lie, but even with that, there was more to the story.

Was there more to the story?

That was what was eating at Cade. Maybe he could live with what happened, even deal with it, if he knew precisely why they'd done it. Never in the two years of friendship with Elias had Cade ever felt so much as a flicker of desire to have his friend's dick in his hand. Yet after one night, one dance, one kiss, Cade had been practically putty in Elias' hand. God save him, he had enjoyed it that night.

But why?

Elias' brow furrowed, darkening his features. "Then when?"

Cade flopped his arms at his side, making a helpless noise. "I don't know Elias, but not now."

"That's not even close to a good answer, and you know it," Elias growled.

Cade's jaw tightened. "You don't get to tell me when I need to talk."

"I get to have a say when you're leaving me to hang out and dry. This is crap, Cade. We can't be okay if you continue to avoid me. I thought maybe letting you have your space might give you time to be okay, but clearly you're in one of your 'need to deal with it but won't' moods."

"Uh, excuse me?"

Elias snorted. "You know what I mean, and you know I know. Something messes with you, and sometimes you need to be left alone to deal with it. Other times, you gotta talk about it and will. And every now and then, you should talk, but you won't, and you act like...*this,* until someone makes you, usually me."

Cade slapped the sponge back down into the soapy bucket. "I don't *need* to talk about anything."

"The hell you don't," Elias shot back, eyes narrowing almost to slits.

"I don't!"

"Fine, be a stubborn dumbass. But *I* do need to talk about it. How about that?"

Cade blinked. "Well...not now!"

"When?"

"I don't know!"

The shriek of the alarm cut through Elias' next retort. They froze as the alarm rose and fell before they shook their surprise off. Cade's frustration evaporated, and he watched as Elias' dark eyes turned away from his face and up toward the alarm. Without needing to say anything, they both moved, heading for their gear.

"Later," Cade said as he pulled open his locker.

"I'm fucking holding you to that," Elias told him as he pulled out the jacket and pants.

THE FLAMES WERE LICKING up at the sky as their truck barreled down the street. People were crowded on the opposite side of the burning building, eyes wide, and mouths constantly moving as they gossiped. The building, built in the style of an old hunting lodge, was puffing out thick clouds of black smoke, blotting out the sun as it rose into the sky.

Cade yanked the radio from its hook and called into it. "Keith, Davis, get to the hoses. Keep it from spreading."

Keith's voice crackled back. "On it."

Cade elbowed Elias beside him. "Us too."

Elias nodded, hopping out of the truck with Cade following suit. Habit and training took over their limbs as they began to work. Thankfully, it wasn't one of those fires where some idiot had blocked the hydrants. While Cade always got a small dose of pleasure from having to break the windows of a car whose owner thought they didn't have to obey the law, he preferred not to have to deal with the screaming later.

They worked quickly, neither of them noticing the sounds of the nearby crowd. Setting up the hose, they got to work. Cade braced, gritting his teeth as the flow of the water worked through the hose. Between he and Elias, though, the hose stayed in one place and didn't rip out of his hands. On his first call, Cade had watched a hose fly out of a man's hand and smack his partner in the face, after seeing the bloody broken nose and bruised face, Cade had made sure to always have a firm grip when he was working.

Elias' voice was thick behind his visor, but audible. "We're going to need more people, this isn't enough."

Cade nodded, but thankfully someone had already called in more than just their station. The building was large and had caught fire quickly. He didn't know what the hell was in that building, but it had apparently caught swiftly. Cade had a feeling the arson specialists would be paying a visit once it was all said and done.

"At least there's nothing close," Cade threw out.

"Yeah."

They managed to douse as much of the surrounding area as they could while also battling the fire at the edges. To his right, he could see Keith and Davis working hard to keep their side under control, but Elias was right. There was no way the four of them were going to be enough to keep the fire down.

"You smell that?" Elias asked.

Cade shook his head. "No, visor kind of ruins it. What?"

"Smells like gas to me."

How the hell Elias could smell anything but smoke and his own sweat was beyond Cade. But after working with the man for two years, Cade knew better than to argue with him. It was a bit of a joke between them that Elias had a super-human sense of smell, though Elias blamed Cade's smoking for his bad nose. If Elias said he smelled gas, then it had probably been used as an accelerant.

Still holding tight to the hose, Cade brought the walkie on his jacket up. "Boys in blue, if you could get the civilians back, way, way back, I would appreciate it."

"Something bad?" a wary sounding voice replied.

"Dunno, but better safe than sorry," Cade said.

He didn't bother looking over his shoulder to check if the police were doing just that. At times like this, the police could only maneuver the crowd back as gently as possible so as not to start a panic. Cade was sure everything would be fine, but if there was gas, there might be some left over that could feed the fire. The last thing they needed was to have a crowd of civilians in their way if they needed more room.

Elias grunted. "Sounds like back up is almost here."

Cade nodded, hearing the rising and falling sirens of incoming trucks. From the sounds of it, there was more than just one station coming to help them. Which was good, old buildings could be tricky to put out with a small, four-man crew. At worst, the fire could engulf the entire thing instead of just eating away at rooms and hallways, sometimes finding flammable surprises along the way.

"Sorry," Elias grunted, adjusting the nozzle head.

"For what? If you smell gas, you smell gas," Cade called to him.

"Not what I meant."

"Then what?"

Elias glanced at him, his face obscured by the sun hitting the visor. "For pushing you. I shouldn't be pushing you, not about this."

Oh, that.

Cade sighed, shaking his head. "No, don't be sorry."

They did need to talk. Cade hated to admit it and might have avoided it completely if Elias hadn't all but pinned him to the wall over it. But having it thrown in his face told him that maybe it was time to find his spine and talk to his friend.

"Look, if you want to talk, just...come find me, alright? I'm sick of not having my best friend, I want Cade back," Elias said, voice tight with focus.

Cade smiled. "Okay."

Then the world exploded.

Hot air slammed into Cade as a massive wall of fire shot into the sky. The wind was knocked from his lungs as he tumbled backward. No air left to grunt, Cade hit the ground soundlessly on his back. Blinking rapidly, he stared up at the sky, now filled with pouring black smoke and fluttering burning pieces of wood and paper.

Cade sucked in his first breath of air, his lungs screaming for oxygen. His body ached, battered by both the invisible blow and his body hitting the ground. His ears rang, and as he strained, he realized he could hear cries and yells, but it was though they were coming from underwater. His mind whirled and hiccupped, trying desperately to figure out what had happened.

Finding his strength, he pushed himself upright and stared at the building, or rather, what was left of it. The roof was entirely gutted, flames and black smoke pouring out of it and into the sky. The windows were all gone, and several walls were missing or had been punched through.

"An explosion?" Cade asked dumbly.

Before he could begin to wonder how it had happened, his gaze fell on a pile of debris nearby. At first, it could have been mistaken for any other pile of wood, plaster, and who knew what else blown away from the house.

Except for the booted foot sticking out from the bottom of the pile.

"Elias!" Cade yelped, scrambling to his feet.

Cade rushed over, heart pounding. There was no movement, no call, nothing from Elias to show that he was alive. Cade smacked the first layers of the pile away, grunting as he had to move larger chunks of wood. When he got to the bottom, he let out a low moan of pain. A thick chunk of what had been a wooden ceiling beam, still smoldering from the fire, lay across Elias' back. Elias himself was unmoving, his face obscured by the visor on his face, and Cade couldn't tell if he was breathing.

"Fuck," Cade grunted, trying to grab hold of the beam in a relatively safe spot and yank it away.

His muscles strained, and he felt it give the slightest inch, and no more. Mentally screaming at himself to stay calm, he looked around frantically for something to help lift the beam up with.

"Cade!"

Davis' voice brought Cade around, and he caught sight of both he and Keith running toward them. They looked unharmed, and a small dose of relief shot through him. Keith was an asshole, and Davis could be just as bad sometimes, but dammit, he was glad they were alive.

"Ax! Get an ax!" Cade barked as they hurried toward him.

Thankfully, Davis veered away, booking it toward one of the trucks without hesitation. Keith jogged up to him, his eyes falling on Elias and let out a groan.

"Shit."

Cade tried to keep himself still, trying to pretend he wasn't standing over his best friend pinned to the ground and possibly dead.

Cade looked at Keith. "Get the EMTs. Davis and I can get him out with the ax."

Keith glanced at him, his visor pulled up, and Cade could see the unspoken question in his eyes. Cade's gaze hardened, and Keith nodded, running toward the crowd. It was only then he realized that people were freaking out. Cries and shouts rang out, and while Cade was sure they were at a much safer distance, he couldn't promise that nothing had flown that far.

He didn't honestly care.

Cade crouched down by Elias' head, gently pulling up the visor as best he could. Elias' eyes were closed, and there was a bruise forming where his head must have smacked against something. But there was breathing, thank God, there was breathing.

"Hold on Elias, don't you fucking die on me," Cade whispered, chest clenching. "Don't you fucking dare."

ELIAS

The first thing he became aware of was beeping. Next came the presence of something in his nose.

Then a dull, burning ache throughout his back.

"Ugh," he managed.

"Elias?"

He tried to say Cade's name, but it came out as another low groan. It felt like someone had railed on his back a few times with a baseball bat. His shoulder was throwing a fit too, and he winced when he tried to move it.

Cade's voice was next to him. "Hey, don't move. You're in the hospital."

He was what?

Forcing himself to open his eyes, he squinted at the bright light coming from the ceiling. The first thing to clear in his vision was Cade's face, pinched with worry even though he was smiling. Elias looked around, blinking as he took in the sight of the pristine walls, the raised bed he lay in, and the medical equipment next to his bed.

"The fuck?" he muttered.

Cade let out a shaky laugh. "Yeah, buddy, that was more or less my reaction too. Jesus Christ, you scared the living shit out of me for a while there."

Elias frowned up at him, reaching up to lay a hand on the side of Cade's neck. There was soot smeared across Cade's cheek and a bandage on the right side of his neck. His skin was sticky from sweat, and he looked more exhausted than Elias had ever seen him.

"What happened?" Elias asked.

Cade leaned on the bed, seemingly unwilling to stop touching Elias. "There was an explosion."

"Oh, good, he's awake," a new voice announced.

Elias turned to the new person, wearing doctor's scrubs and a coat. He was an older man, probably in his mid to late forties. While Elias was no expert on good looking man, the doctor was certainly a handsome man. His black hair, kept short, was sprinkled with white, and he was a little gray around the temples as well. Bright blue eyes crinkled at the corners of a well-formed face, a strong jaw, and the nose which looked previously broken to Elias only added a little bit of charm.

"Good evening, I'm Doctor Andrews. It's nice to see you awake, Elias," the doctor said as he looked him over.

"Awake but a little confused," Elias admitted.

"I was starting to explain," Cade said.

The doctor nodded. "It seems there was an explosion at the fire you were helping to put out. The blast wasn't too bad, but you and your partner here were close enough to get knocked off your feet. And you were unlucky enough to end up buried under rubble."

"Would that explain my back?" Elias asked with a wince.

"That it would. Seems a large beam fell on you. Honestly, from the sounds of it, you're a very lucky man. That beam could have easily killed you. Now, this is only a guess, but I suspect it hit the ground, where most of the force went. You did, however, take quite a beating in the process."

Elias flopped his head back. "What's broken and how long am I stuck in bed?"

"We're still making sure you're okay, but all in all, you're a lucky man with only a few bruises."

"Feels like more than a few," Elias grumbled.

Doctor Andrews chuckled. "Yes, I imagine it does. You'll find that your back is going to hurt for a while, but we'll give you something for it."

Elias waved a hand. "Don't."

Cade squeezed his arm gently. "Elias."

"I'm not dealing with pain killers. Those things fuck you up."

"This really isn't the time to be stubborn. You almost died, dumbass."

Elias looked at him, scowling. "And I'm not having my body freak out because it wants drugs. And who are you calling a dumbass? You're the one sitting there bandaged up and not having taken a shower."

Cade snorted. "I've been here, waiting for you to wake up. Dumbass."

Doctor Andrews listened, a smile pulling at his mouth. "Well, now that we've established that. By all accounts, you should be out in the next day or two. Would you say no to, not a pain killer, but a reliever? I'm sure we can scrounge up some ibuprofen for you, with a little more kick than the over the counter sort."

"That I won't say no to," Elias admitted.

Doctor Andrews shoved his hands in his pockets. "Good, then I'll send a nurse in to give you your pills. You should at least try to get some rest in the meantime."

"Isn't that what I have been doing?" Elias asked.

"Try for some more then."

Elias nodded, not willing to argue. He didn't feel like getting up and going anywhere anyway. His back hurt, but at least it wasn't pure agony. And he didn't care if Cade was going to bitch at him, he didn't hurt enough to need pain killers.

When the doctor left, Cade scowled at him. "Why didn't you just take the damn pain killers?"

"Because I don't need them."

"A big ass beam fell on you, Elias."

"And apparently they're going to let me go tomorrow or the day after. If I was hurt *that* bad, I wouldn't be getting released so quickly. And last I checked, I know my own pain tolerance."

"You're still being stubborn."

Elias decided it was time for a new subject. "How the hell did it blow up?"

Cade frowned, shaking his head. "I don't know. One minute we were doing our thing, and the next minute I was on my back, wondering what the fuck just happened. Best we can guess, there was a live gas line in the basement of the building."

Elias frowned. "Shouldn't we have known that beforehand?"

"Gas company swears up and down that there was no gas approved to go there. Place has been for sale for months now, and there's not even water running to it."

"Weird."

"Yeah, I'm sure they'll be looking into it."

"How are Keith and Davis?"

"Barely touched. They weren't as close as we were."

Elias reached out, gingerly touching the bandage on Cade's neck. "And you?"

Cade smiled, patting Elias' stomach carefully. "Just a little tossed around is all, nothing serious. The bandage is from getting you out from under the beam, nothing big."

"Uh-huh."

"Davis and I used one of the axes as leverage to pull the beam off you and toss it aside. It broke something in the pile of shit we threw it on, and something flew out and winged me. Seriously, it's fine."

"The 'needed to be bandaged' kinda fine?" Elias asked doubtfully.

"If I can't argue with you about the pain killers, then you can't argue with me about this."

Elias huffed. "Stubborn."

Cade caught his wrist, squeezing it. "Back at ya."

"Thanks for pulling me out," Elias said.

Cade leaned forward, pressing his forehead to Elias'. "Every time."

Elias nodded, closing his eyes and enjoying the contact. After the week he'd had, it was nice to have this moment with Cade, even if it had come at the cost of his back for a little while. Yet even amongst that, he could feel Cade's warm skin and his breath on Elias' lips.

Oh.

Elias chuckled. "You're sticky and smell of smoke, dude."

"I know, I probably reek of sweat too," Cade said with a smile, slowly pulling away.

Elias suddenly hated their lack of contact. "Go take a shower. I'll still be here when you come back. And eat too, I know you haven't done that."

Cade hesitated. "I could just…"

Elias interrupted him. "No. Go take care of yourself, I'm going to get some rest. Don't worry about me."

"Good luck on that," Cade muttered but stood up.

Elias watched him leave, his heart pounding as he lay in the room, wondering what had just happened. He could still feel the phantom sensation of Cade's breath upon him, and the desire to close the distance that last inch.

"Wasn't just a one-time thing then," Elias muttered, rubbing his mouth.

Or maybe he could just blame the fact that he almost died. But no, that wouldn't work either. How many times was he going to be tempted to blame it on anything else but what it was? Maybe just once blaming it on the booze would have worked, even though the sensations had sat with him for days afterward.

He had to be honest with himself, laying there in a hospital bed after almost getting himself blown up. Elias loved touching Cade, always had enjoyed their physical affection. Now it had taken on a whole new meaning, and he wished that he could convince Cade to let go of all his hang-ups and just...lay with him.

Instead, he was left to think, alone in the room, about his life and about what came next.

* * *

ELIAS WASN'T surprised when Cade reappeared a few hours later. Night had already fallen, and the lights in the room were kept low in case Elias wanted to sleep. Which was rather pointless, in his opinion, since he'd been sleeping off and on the whole time. He'd also spent his time awake thinking over everything, punctuated by drifting off to sleep. By the time Cade showed up again, Elias knew exactly what he was going to say.

Cade came in, wearing a t-shirt and a pair of jeans, and Elias realized he'd never paid attention to how Cade dressed. His clothes were never flashy or expensive, but he somehow managed to always look put together. His clothes weren't tight, but they hugged him, hinting at the flat stomach and the built chest. It wasn't Elias' favorite sight, but on Cade, he found he was growing to like it.

"Hey, you're awake," Cade said, beaming.

"For the moment. I keep drifting off," Elias said, watching Cade's every movement.

"I wanted to stop in before they chased me out," Cade said, glancing toward the door.

Elias chuckled. "Scared of the big bad nurses?"

"You don't piss off nurses dude, you just don't."

"Tell me about it. I was raised by one."

"Oh, right. Oh shit, have you called your mom?"

Elias winced. "I'll call her tomorrow. They told me they didn't call her, so I get to be the one to deliver the news. Which is...fun."

Cade sat at the edge of the bed, smirking. "At least as a nurse, she should be alright."

"She's also my mother, so she'll not be okay."

"I think mine would be more worried if it would throw off her social schedule."

Elias wrinkled his nose, never liking the topic of Pamela. "Speaking of, have you heard from her?"

"It's uh, actually been a couple of days, which is weird for her. I'm starting to wonder if something happened to her."

"But not enough for you to find out."

"Fuck no."

Elias laughed, reaching out to take Cade's hand in his. Cade watched him, allowing his hand to be held and to even give a light squeeze in return. There was a reluctance in the action from Cade that Elias didn't miss. Cade's eyes didn't quite want to meet his, and Elias felt his heart squeeze.

"Elias," Cade began.

Elias shook his head. "Just, let me talk. You don't have to talk. Let me say what I want to say, and then you can take the time you need to think through it and tell me what you want in your own time, okay?"

Cade looked wary but nodded.

Elias took a deep breath. "I've had a bit of time to think about this, and maybe getting blown up shook a few thoughts loose. But here's the thing, I'm not...sorry that it happened."

Cade finally looked up.

Elias continued. "I'll be sorry, more sorry than I've ever been if it ruins our friendship. Our friendship means everything to me, Cade, you're my best friend. But I also don't think that...that this is something that has to get in the way."

"How?" Cade asked softly.

Elias tried to smile. "By being honest about it, by confronting it. What happened that night was...not what I expected. Hell, I sat around all day Sunday, wondering what the ever-living fuck we'd done."

"I sense a 'but' somewhere in there."

"But, you know me, I can't not be honest with myself, and I'm going to be just as honest with you. I...liked what happened."

Cade's eyes widened, but he said nothing.

"And I know, that's kind of weird. We're both straight guys, and what happened shouldn't have, and we shouldn't have enjoyed it. But I did. And I've had to admit that to myself over the past week. And I've had plenty of time to sit on it the past few hours. Now I'm noticing things like how bright your eyes are, how good you look in those clothes, and feeling like I want to kiss you when you get close to me."

"You...want to do more?" Cade asked.

Elias shrugged. "I think so, well, no, I'm feeling the temptation too. But the thing is, I need you to be on board too. If you're on board for that, if you're okay with it, and want to try more. I'm there for it. But my...wondering what it would be like, to be with you, to be something more than *just* friends isn't enough for me to throw our friendship away either, Cade. So yeah, I'm into...more, but more importantly, I want Cade back, as I said before. So you think, and you tell me when you're ready to talk, okay?"

He'd said what he'd intended to say, and there was nothing else that could be done. Cade hadn't bolted from the room immediately, so Elias took that as a good sign. Slowly though, Cade pulled his hand back and stood up.

"Okay," he said with a nod. "I'll...think. About what you said and about...the other stuff."

Elias knew he was leaving. Cade had to go think, and as much as it pained him to watch his friend go, Elias knew it was for the best. Elias watched him go, heart heavy as Cade slipped out of the room.

Elias closed his eyes, forcing himself to take a deep breath. He'd put himself out there, now he needed to only wait to find out Cade's verdict.

CADE

*H*e'd slept like absolute shit, and he knew he looked like it too. At least twice, a passing nurse had asked him if he was feeling well. Both times, Cade had flashed them what he hoped was a winning smile and told them he was fine, just hungover. One had scowled at him and told him to be more responsible and make sure not to make too much noise in the ward, and the other had smiled knowingly before walking off. Different reactions, but at least they'd both resulted in him being left alone.

Cade had been sitting in the small waiting room since about six in the morning. After he'd left Elias' room the night before, Cade had tried to go back to his apartment and get some sleep. He should have known better than to have such high hopes and had spent most of the night staring up at his ceiling.

Elias' words still bounced around in his head, crowding together before ricocheting somewhere else. In some ways, he wasn't really surprised to find that Elias was so utterly calm about the entire thing. The man was so goddamn unflappable, though it wasn't usually so unnerving. For someone who'd spent their whole life as a straight man, Elias was ready to take the leap into...into what?

What the hell could Cade even call what Elias was feeling, what *he* was feeling? Did Cade share Elias' feelings? Yeah, okay, he did. But how did that make any sense? Neither of them had any right to be feeling anything toward one another that was sexual or romantic.

Yet just as Elias had said it about himself, Cade couldn't deny, to himself at least, that he'd liked what had happened. And now he was wondering not only what it meant, but he had Elias' words about 'more' stuck in his head too. More, like what? Kissing, groping, fondling...fucking?

Cade's stomach clenched as his mind ran away with that thought. Images of Elias' hard, naked body, hovering above him. Elias' mouth against his neck, kissing and licking him, throwing in a playful nip here and there. And the feel of Elias inside him, or him inside Elias.

The thoughts were not exactly making it easier. And especially because they were having an effect on the front of his pants, he didn't need to be having in public.

Pushing himself out of his seat, he got up to get more coffee. As he passed by Elias' room, he glanced in and found the man still sleeping. Cade lingered in the doorway for a moment, leaning in to watch. He knew from one of the nurses that Elias had got up a few times in the middle of the night to use the bathroom, and despite a little bit of wincing, professed that he was fine. Cade wasn't so sure about that, but he also knew there was no point in arguing with Elias when he got that stony look on his face.

"What am I going to do with you?" Cade asked softly before walking off.

He came back a few minutes later with a fresh cup of coffee. If he wasn't careful, he was going to end up an addict just like Elias was. Then again, maybe Elias just drank it because he was so damn tired all the time. Cade could finally sympathize, his sleep the past week had been absolute shit.

Cade slumped back in his seat, wondering if he might try for a little nap. That changed immediately as he heard the oh so familiar, and not so dulcet tones of his mother. Cade shot forward in his seat, leaning to look into the hallway where the nurses' station sat. Sure enough, Pamela Masters, adorned in her standard pantsuit and a large hat perched atop her head, stood talking to one of the nurses.

"Mother?" Cade asked, bewildered.

"Oh, there's my son. Never mind, dear, you've been no help anyway," Pamela told the disgruntled looking nurse behind the counter.

Cade shot her an apologetic look. He hadn't caught the conversation they'd been having, but considering his mother, he was sure it hadn't been fun. Great, just what he needed, for him to be associated with his mother to the nurses, and so putting Elias in a bad light.

Pamela hustled into the waiting room. "I have honestly been run all over this hospital in the hopes of finding you. Not one person had any idea what they were talking about, I've been here for over an hour."

Cade raised a brow and had to repress the urge to snort. Somehow he got the feeling that the people his mother had spoken to had known precisely what they were talking about when they'd led her astray. Every now and then, his mother ran into a problem, at a store usually, where she was led on a wild goose chase. It had yet to occur to her that it wasn't due to incompetence, but the petty revenge of people in customer service who had to tolerate pushy, condescending people like Pamela Masters every day.

"Okay, that answers what you're doing, but not why. Why are you here?" Cade asked.

"Well, I need a reason to look for my son?" she asked.

"You shouldn't even know I'm here," Cade pointed out.

"Of course you're here, that man, Elliot, is here."

Cade narrowed his eyes. "Elias."

"Yes, him. So, of course, you're here. Now come along, we had a tea scheduled for today."

Cade groaned. "Mother, today is...really not a good day. This week is really not a good week. I can do it next weekend."

"Next weekend simply will not do. I have a luncheon with William and a cocktail party with the Cyders."

"Then the weekend after that."

"Kaidan Masters, you can spare to pull yourself away from...here, for a couple of hours."

Cade took another step back, heat rising to his face. "Don't say 'here' when you mean 'him.' And no, I'm not 'pulling myself away' from Elias. I'm all he's got right now, and he's not in the hospital because he stubbed his toe. He almost got blown up."

"And yet clearly, if he's in this ward, he'll be fine," Pamela added with a light huff.

Cade gripped the cup of coffee in his hand, telling himself repeatedly that he should not lose his temper. The past week had been the roughest, most confusing one he could remember, and it had culminated in the scare of his life. If he wanted to sit around the hospital like a creep, making sure his best friend really was okay and had someone by his side, then by God, he was going to do it.

Cade took a deep breath. "And like I said, his family isn't here, and I'm all he has at the moment. I'm not leaving him alone."

"Is he even awake?"

"No, but he might be soon."

"Might."

"Yes, Mother, might. And when he does, I want him to see a face that he recognizes and cares about."

Her eyes narrowed. "So it's true."

Cade's heart skipped. "What?"

"I didn't want to believe it. When Stephan tried to tell me, I told him that my Kaidan would *never* enter into a...a relationship with another man," Pamela said, her voice rising ever so slightly from her outrage.

"Stephan?" What the hell would the guy who collected cars and women like trading cards know about Cade's social life?

"Yes, apparently he heard it over a few drinks with the Danvers. I have no idea where they heard it, he didn't know. I told him it was just gossip, but as I live and breathe, I'm finding out it's true..." Pamela continued, gripping her wrist as though to hold herself back.

"Mother," Cade began, trying to wrap his head around the fact that his mother knew about his and Elias' little charade.

"And look at you, you're not even trying to deny it!" she continued, eyes flashing.

Considering how quiet she had been, he probably should have suspected that this was her problem. Despite her apparent refusal to accept it when told, she'd still been avoiding Cade. He couldn't help but think of the parallels between that and what he'd been doing to Elias.

Pamela drew herself up stiffly at his silence. "And to make matters worse. You're dating *him*?"

Cade straightened as well. "What, excuse me? What did you just say?"

Pamela whispered fiercely. "It's one thing for you to sleep with all those women like some common man whore. And I might have been able to tolerate some little fling with another man, God knows it's a different era. But to slum it as well? Kaidan, I raised you better than that."

Cade's mouth fell open. "Slum it?"

"What else would you call this? I was against this so-called friendship from the very beginning, but I had hoped you'd have the sense to know when to cut your losses. Instead, you're now...shacking up with him?" Pamela asked.

Cade stared at her, barely able to keep up with her words as she spat them out. He'd always known that she wasn't the biggest fan of his friendship with Elias or Elias in general. Yet he'd never quite fathomed just how much she had positively loathed the man, how much she seemed to hate him.

"Stop," he whispered.

"No, Kaidan, I will *not* stop. I have had quite enough of all of this. You are not dating that...man anymore, and you are done with all this nonsense. You have had your fun for years now, and it is high time you came back and behaved like a proper member of the Masters family!"

Enough.

"Shut your fucking mouth, Mother," Cade said, his voice filled with grim wonder.

Pamela jerked as though slapped. "What did you say?"

Cade gave an ugly laugh. "I told you what I should have told you years ago. Shut your fucking mouth."

"How dare you..."

Cade cut across her with a sudden snarl. "No, how dare *you*. How dare you barge into my life and think you have any say in what I do or don't do, who I'm friends with, and who I'm sleeping with. And how dare you think you have any right to say anything about someone I might or might not be dating."

Pamela's eyes brightened briefly. "So you're not..."

Cade sneered at her. "And more importantly, how dare you talk about a man who is a better person than you could ever dream of being. How dare you talk about Elias as if you have the right. Elias is a good man, he's honest, tough, and he never forgets his heart. I know that's hard for you to under-stand since you left yours half-rotted and buried in some ditch somewhere."

Pamela's eyes practically bulged out of her head. "Kaidan Masters! You will *not* speak to me…"

He ignored her. "And before you even think about threat-ening me, take the allowance. Take the money. As a matter of fact, I don't fucking want it anymore. I don't want *you* anymore. I'm perfectly happy living off the money I make working at the station. Working with the men who are like a family in their own way, and with Elias, who loves me and who I love more than my own goddamn family ever has."

Cade's head spun with his anger, with the words flying out of his mouth like flaming knives. The part of him that kept himself in check, that kept his mouth in control while speaking to his mother was gone. It had burned up in the sudden rage at the culmination of his mother's insults, condescension, and every nasty little thing she had thrown at him to bring him down, to bring him to heel.

"And when I'm with him, I'll think about the miserable life you had planned for me, that you've done to yourself. All those fake smiles, those little laughs, pretending you like all the snakes you stab in the back when they're not looking. All those rich parties with awful people, pretending all the money in the world makes you all so great. Well, you know what *Pamela*, I don't want it, and I won't have it. Write me out of the will, pretend you don't have a son, because, at this point, you might as well not!"

His voice had risen, echoing down the halls. People were peering out of their rooms, and even the nurses were looking around the corner at them. Elias stood at the door to his own room, standing strong, his eyes riveted on Cade's face. Cade looked at him, nodding his head in the hopes that it said he meant everything he said.

Pamela followed his gaze, and her eyes narrowed.

"Don't you say a word to him. Get the fuck out of here, Pamela," Cade barked.

She turned to look at Cade once more, her chin wobbling, but finally, she turned and marched out. Even insulted publicly and humiliated, she held her head high as she left. Cade didn't care if she believed she still held onto her dignity. He didn't even care that he felt sick to his stomach. Cade had finally let out everything he'd been holding in, and he wasn't going to regret it, no matter what his mother tried to throw at him.

Cade ignored the looks of everyone else and walked to Elias. "What are you doing up?"

Elias smirked. "I have a sore, bruised back, not a broken one. They're letting me out today."

"When?" Cade asked.

"In a couple of hours. They've got paperwork to do," Elias said.

"When did they tell you that?"

"You were sleeping in the waiting room."

Cade blinked. "Oh. I didn't know that you…"

Elias chuckled, wrapping an arm around Cade's shoulders and pulled him in. "I knew you were here, keeping an eye on me."

Cade hugged him back, wishing he could hold him tight. Instead, he clung to the man that was his best friend, the man who understood him and loved him for who he was. And hell, maybe the waters between them were muddied as hell, but he could deal with that.

Elias pressed a kiss to the top of Cade's head. "Go."

Cade looked up. "What?"

"I know you need to breathe, to walk off what just happened."

"I'm not…" Cade began.

Elias smirked. "You wanna, and you know it. You've got a couple of hours. I'll text you when they let me out, I promise. You can be my taxi."

Cade looked over him, frowning. "Promise?"

"I promise."

Cade backed away. "Okay, I'll be back."

And he meant it, in every way he possibly could.

CADE

Cade's fingers shook as he brought the cup of tea to his lips, his mind so caught up in the fury of his thoughts he didn't notice the people around him at the cafe. Had he really told his mother to basically fuck off? It wasn't like it was the first time he'd wanted to, but he'd always clamped down on his tongue and bore through her bullshit.

Cade still didn't know *how* he felt about Elias, but he knew damn well he wasn't going to listen to her speak about him like that either. Cade knew full well that Pamela Masters had never liked Elias, and disapproved heavily of Cade's close friendship with the man. None of that excused the god awful, gut-wrenching, cruel things she'd said. His sexuality was up for question, not his loyalty.

"Damn her," he hissed.

A shadow fell over him, forcing him to look up into the face of one of the last people he wanted to see at that moment.

Christine chuckled lightly. "My, my, I never took you for the sort to drink tea, Cade. You continue to be full of surprises."

"Oh Christ, not now, Christine," he snarled.

Her thin brow shot up. "Oh? Having a rough day?"

"I'm having a rough fucking time in general, no thanks to you, and no thanks to my goddamn mother. So maybe you can come back another time when I feel up to doing the stupid subtle jabbing back and forth thing you're so fond of. Because right now, all I'm willing to do is tell you to fuck off with your games and go back to your goddamn penthouse while you plot out how to ruin my life even further," he spat furiously at her.

That was about the point he expected her claws to come out, and she'd give him another target to take his anger out on. To his complete surprise, she tilted her head, her expression softening. Reaching out, she waved to someone in the cafe behind him, before placing herself carefully in the seat across from him.

"What are you doing?" Cade demanded.

"Tell me what's going on," she said, placing her white, gold-trimmed wallet before her carefully.

"Why?"

"Because you obviously need to talk about it."

"What about my face, my words, my *anything*, says I need to talk?"

"All of it. For all the faults Pamela might lay at your feet, you're not a man to react with cruelty or out of anger. If you're willing to lash out at me, I would say that's a strong indication something is clearly bothering you."

Cade narrowed his eyes. "Been speaking to my mother again? Have a nice little chat?"

She laughed softly. "Please, no one speaks *with* your mother. They listen to her and simply throw in a word here and there to make her think they're listening. But yes, she's spoken to me a handful of times over the past week. She's not terribly happy with you, and from the sounds of it, the feeling is mutual."

It was the realization that Christine treated his mother much like Cade did that cooled the sharper edges of his anger more than anything. He continued to stare at her, trying to figure out what it was she wanted and what her angle was. A server appeared at his side, dropping a steaming cup of something on the table in front of her, and then slipping away as Christine murmured her thanks.

"This, what is this?" Cade asked, motioning to her, and then to himself.

Christine arched a delicate brow as she brought the cup up to blow on it gently. "This is called concern, Cade."

"Since when?"

"Rudeness again, I see."

"You play games, Christine. We both know that, let's not pretend."

Christine took a small sip, sighing contentedly as she set the cup back. "True, very true. I won't sit here and pretend otherwise."

"Including trying to catch Elias and me in some sort of lie."

"Also true."

"And threatening our jobs if you don't get what you want."

She paused, tilting her head gently to one side. Her brow creased as she looked him over.

"False," she said softly.

Cade blinked. "What?"

"False. I had no intention of causing you to lose your job, Cade, nor do I have any intention of bringing harm to your friend. I approached you months ago because I was interested in you. Your continued attempts to evade me were amusing, though less so when Pamela became involved. In truth, I've been waiting for you to simply, what's the phrase, sack up, and tell me the God honest truth."

"You...what?"

Christine laughed. "Honestly, Cade, despite how amusing it all was, I was growing a little irritated that you wouldn't be honest with me. At least if you were, I could tell Pamela it wasn't going to happen, and it would have spared us both the hassle. Instead, you had to drag it out with various excuses, culminating in this latest falsehood."

Cade stared at her, disbelieving. "You...then, why do all this shit? Why tell the Chief and make him think you were going to make life hard on him if we were found out as liars? Why throw that stupid fucking party?"

Christine shrugged. "Because this last lie was just so...ridiculous, I couldn't help myself. You'd repeatedly been making this harder than it needed to be, so I admit, I wanted to see how far you'd take it. Of course, I never expected...is that why you're so angry?"

"My mother," Cade hissed at her.

Christine winced. "Ah, yes, of course. Not my finest moment. And the one where I've clearly gone too far. Honestly, I wasn't thinking things through. As you said, I enjoy my games, and this one went further than I meant it. But I can promise you, you were never in any danger from me."

Which made him feel as relieved as the proverbial man who goes from fryer to freezer would. Now Cade was left with the realization that everything he'd done, everything he and Elias had gone through, was because he'd been too scared of telling Christine the truth. Even worse, it had also happened because he'd been so sure Christine was out to get him.

"Fuck," he muttered, rubbing at his face.

Christine watched him. "It is because of what I did, isn't

it? I'm so sorry Cade, I never meant for that to happen. I'll personally explain it to Pamela myself, and Chief Irons for that matter."

Cade snorted, shaking his head. "My mother has bigger issues with me right now than that."

She nodded in understanding. "I see I'm not the only one who faced your acid tongue today."

"No, and she's...well, what's done is done."

Instead, he had a bigger problem. Despite hating watching his life slowly fall apart before his eyes, he was more worried about his...friendship, relationship, whatever the hell it was called, between him and Elias. Everything had happened so fast, and he still wasn't sure what he was supposed to think and feel. Now he had the chance to finally be free of it, to have he and Elias go back to where they'd started.

But did he really want to?

"I don't want to date you," he blurted.

"Color me surprised," she said dryly.

"And I wasn't dating Elias."

"I see. Was that so hard?"

"Not now. Not when there's bigger problems."

"Like Pamela?"

"Like..."

He hesitated for only a moment, and then it spilled out of him. The ease of their friendship and the casualness of their contact and affection for one another. The way things had begun to change rapidly, making them more aware of every little thing they did. Sometimes it was just awkward, and sometimes it was awkward because it was even more comforting.

Then the night of her so-called congratulatory party.

It was then that Christine's eyes widened slightly, but to her credit, she showed only mild surprise and listened attentively. Cade skated over the intimate details of that night but made sure she knew that more had happened than in two years of friendship. How they were left to drift apart, while still pretending in public, never really knowing what that night meant.

How even the fire, and how badly it had struck the fear of God into Cade to have almost lost his friend, hadn't done anything more than confuse him further. He was a man who'd been firmly in the heterosexual camp his whole life, but now he was finding himself wanting someone else. And not just someone else, his very straight friend, who seemed more interested in the strange attraction that had seemingly sprung up overnight, than Cade himself was.

When he was done, he was left to stare at his half-drunk, cold cup of tea. He realized he'd never actually put everything into words before, having left everything to stew away in his head for days. And he certainly hadn't expected to tell the whole story to Christine of all people.

Christine took a deep breath, then let it out slowly. "That was...quite the story Cade."

"It's true. Every word of it," Cade said hurriedly.

"Oh, I don't doubt for an instant that this is the most honest you've ever been with me. And I also don't doubt for an instant that everything you've been feeling toward Elias is completely genuine," she said.

Cade snorted, taking a hasty drink. "Right, the lifelong bachelor, womanizer, Kaidan Masters, is suddenly into his best friend, who for the record, is also straight."

Christine shook her head, tapping the metal table gently. "You're focusing too much on whether or not it makes sense, not whether it feels right. Are you honestly so hung up on your heterosexuality? Is that it?"

Cade wrinkled his nose. "This isn't about being against gay guys."

"Well, no, I imagine not. When I spoke to Chief Irons the night of the party, he was adamant that you and Elias have both been particularly good when it comes to your gay co-worker."

"Well, yeah. Matt's a good guy."

"But...?"

Cade scowled. "It's a little different when suddenly you find two straight guys wanting to...do not so straight things."

"I believe you can just come right out and say that you're experiencing a sexual and romantic attraction to Elias."

"Geez, Christine, if you're going to be that blunt, you might as well just say 'fuck and date' while you're at it."

She chuckled. "The end result is the same."

"And the result is hard to wrap my brain around."

Christine ran a finger around the rim of her cup. "Look, I'll make it simple. Do you care about him?"

"Yes."

"Do you want him to be in your life for the rest of your lives?"

"Damn right."

"Do you share your lives with one another and want to continue to do it?"

"Yep."

"And does being around him, spending time with him, showing affection, physical and otherwise, make you feel good, happy, and content?"

Cade's mouth worked before finally nodding. "Yes."

Christine smiled wide. "And, are you sexually attracted to him?"

Cade's mouth slammed shut, and he brought his eyes back to the tabletop between them. His cheeks burned, but he continued to keep his silence as he tried to figure out how he wanted to answer that.

It wasn't like he hadn't been thinking about that night

since it happened. It had been so different, feeling so much strength in the grip of someone holding onto him. How it had been so weird, yet somehow natural, to dance and grind with Elias as they'd tried to put on a show for the masses. Then had come the kiss. What should have been awkward, had instead left Cade feeling dizzy and off-balance.

Then they'd been alone. And sure, Cade had no doubt the alcohol in their system had played a part, but he couldn't sit there and pretend it was just that. No, it may have been the catalyst, the thing that pushed them over the edge, away from their inhibitions. Elias' mouth on his, holding them tightly together as they pushed, ground, and finally shot over the edge into...well, probably one of the better orgasms Cade had ever had.

Did he want that again? Did he want to strip Elias of his clothes carefully, or maybe even roughly? Did he want to feel Elias' mouth on his body once again, maybe even lower than it had been before?

Christ, did he want to know what it felt like to have Elias inside him, and for him to be inside Elias?

Cade answered the only way he could.

"Yes."

It was soft, but the impact of the admission rocked him. He'd been flinging himself internally, back and forth, between wanting to admit his feelings, new and strange as they were, and desperately trying to get back to normalcy. In all that time, never once had he laid out exactly what he'd been feeling, only sensing it at the edge of his thoughts and hurriedly running away from it.

Christine parted her hands, smiling again. "Then I suppose you have your answer. You have everything you need to take the step of making your lie to me into the truth. If he wants it, and you want it, then that's all you need. Everything else is just an existential crisis."

"That sounds so...middle school," Cade protested.

Christine chuckled, shrugging her thin shoulders. "We all have our own existential crises from time to time. From what Pamela has told me, you've spent most of your adult life knowing what you wanted, which wasn't what your family wanted. And what you didn't want, which was the life you had before. Now you've just hit a point where what you thought you should want, and what you actually want, have clashed in the middle."

Cade smiled. "So, I'm being dramatic and stupid?"

"Of course, you're human. We're all stupid and dramatic creatures, it's in our nature. That doesn't make it wrong."

Cade pushed his cup away. "You know, I never once pictured that it would be you who would make me feel better about this."

"And never once did I picture my little joke would spiral into this. Then again, if this all works out for the two of you, maybe I'll feel a little less guilty."

Cade stood up. "Just...don't let it go completely.

Christine gave him a bright smile, perhaps the truest one he'd seen from her. "No. One must learn from their mistakes. Even if the results turn out well."

Before leaving, he bent down, kissing her on the cheek gently. "Thank you, Christine. You gave me a lot to think about."

Christine winked, picking her teacup up once again. "Go and think, Cade, take the time you need to learn how to deal with what you've just said. But one last piece of advice, if I may be so bold?"

Cade stopped. "What's that?"

She met his gaze. "Maybe, don't leave him out of the process. Talk to him too."

ELIAS

*A*s promised, Cade had dropped him off and got him settled in. His friend had been quiet the whole time, but Elias wasn't surprised. Cade had been through a lot in the past week, and not just because he'd told his mother off. The scene played through in Elias' mind, both elating him and breaking his heart. Cade had stood by Elias, against his mother, but Elias knew it had taken a lot out of him.

Cade had hovered quietly for most of the day, but at one point, had gone for a walk. Elias wasn't surprised, though he'd got a little worried as an hour turned into two. As if on cue, Cade had texted him to tell him he was fine, he'd be back later, and finally, that they would talk.

Not that it exactly went anyway toward easing Elias' mind, but still, it was better than nothing. He wasn't completely sure what Cade meant about them talking, but he wasn't going to press Cade either. Elias had already laid out how he felt, and he'd been witness to Cade's explosion at his mother. All in all, he bet Cade had a lot to think about, and probably even more to talk about.

Despite swearing up and down that he was fine, the chief

point blank refused to let him come back. Elias had been threatened with suspension if he tried to go back to the station before he was allowed. So instead, he'd watched more TV than he could stand, and called his mother half a dozen times.

He was out of things to do.

A knock on his door brought his head up. He was sprawled across his couch, staring up at the ceiling, paying no attention to the TV. It was already late in the evening, and he didn't have one clue who the hell would be visiting him so late. Grunting, he heaved himself off the couch, wincing at the twinge in his shoulder from where the beam had landed on him. It was still bruised, but at least he'd been lucky not to seriously hurt himself.

Elias opened the door and blinked. "Cade?"

"Uh, hi," Cade said, staring at the door as if it were the first time he'd seen it.

"What...are you doing here?"

"Uh, seeing you?"

"No, I mean, why are you knocking? You have a key."

"Yeah, that kind of occurred to me only after I'd knocked."

Elias shook his head, opening the door further and stepping back. "Well, come on in."

Cade did as he was bid, shuffling into the entranceway and past Elias. Closing the door, Elias stopped when he realized Cade hadn't gone much further into the apartment. In fact, the other man was only a foot from him, staring down at his own feet.

"Uh, Cade?" Elias asked slowly.

Cade continued to stare at his feet. "Sorry, it's been so...weird. I meant to stop by and see you, but I've been...thinking."

"Yeah, that's what you said," Elias said, not sure what he was supposed to do.

Cade was just standing there. Elias had figured they had a lot to talk about when Cade finally showed up, but he never realized how hard it must have been on Cade to get to this point.

Elias hoped to make it a little easier. "Look, I know what I said. And I meant it, I did. At the same time, that doesn't mean you have to do anything about it. If you're not wanting to, then that's fine. We can stop being awkward about the whole thing and start being friends again. I just...want you back in my life Cade."

Cade finally looked up, his hazel eyes wide. Elias looked down at him, realizing how close they were and wondered if he should give his friend some space. He froze when Cade reached up, laying a hand on Elias' shoulder and pulling him close. Before Elias could do much more than bend forward out of shock, Cade's lips were on his.

Elias sucked in a sharp breath, stiffening as Cade pushed their mouths firmly together. And there it was again, that same zinging jolt that he'd felt the last two times they'd kissed. The only difference was that Cade was the one who started it, and they were stone-cold sober. Elias couldn't smell any liquor on Cade's breath, and hell, he knew what Cade looked and acted like when he was drinking. No, this was a purely undiluted decision, and Elias' heart began racing feverishly.

Cade pulled back, smiling weakly. "Sorry, I had to...had to know."

Elias blinked, a little surprised still. In some way, despite everything he'd said in the hospital room, Elias hadn't been totally sure if the first time hadn't been a fluke. Having had Cade's lips on him again, admittedly with Elias not participating too much.

"Um, know what?" Elias asked.

Cade snorted softly. "Whether or not what I felt that first time was real or...alcohol induced."

Elias hesitated. "And?"

Cade wrinkled his nose, reaching down to press down on his pants. It took Elias a moment to realize he could see the bulge of Cade's cock. Apparently, the kiss had been more than just a fluke for both of them.

Elias couldn't help but laugh. "Jesus, Cade, you have such a way with words."

Cade scowled. "It was less embarrassing to show you than to say it."

"I mean, I guess?"

Cade reached out and poked Elias' cock. "I'm not alone."

Elias sucked in a breath at the brief contact. Okay, fine. Yes, he had begun to stiffen, but now it was even worse after Cade decided to touch it.

Elias shook his head. "So what, we're...just going to deal with us being into one another now?"

"I mean, it's a little weird...okay, a lot weird. I just got hard from kissing you, and then I poked your hard dick, and I liked it. There's a lot of liking of things I never thought I'd like before," Cade admitted.

"So, where does that leave us?" Elias asked cautiously.

Cade turned his eyes up to him, and Elias blinked, caught off guard by the intensity of them. He'd caught a glimpse of it when he'd kissed Cade the night of the party, and after he'd danced with him. Elias had never quite appreciated how bright Cade's eyes really were, and that was even more apparent now that he had a fire burning behind them.

"Did you really mean everything you said?" Cade asked.

"I told you I did, that hasn't changed," Elias said with a frown.

"You want to see if there's more?"

"I...think it's worth seeing through, if you want."

"And what if we like it?"

"What if we do?"

"Do we start dating?"

Elias cocked his head. "I...hell, Cade, why not?"

Cade leaned back. "Seriously?"

"If we end up liking all this stuff for real, the kissing, the touching, the...whatever else..."

"Butt stuff?" Cade asked with a grin.

"As tactful as ever," Elias said with a smirk.

"I've done butt stuff."

"Cade."

"No, I mean, like, on the receiving end."

The gave Elias pause. "What?"

Cade shrugged. "Some girls are into doing stuff like that. It's not gay or anything. But I've had toys and stuff. Feels good."

Elias wasn't quite sure what he was supposed to say to that. Now he suddenly had the idea of putting something else entirely into Cade's ass. Once more, he found himself thinking that should have been a weird thought, not an arousing one. And yet there he was, getting hard all over again. A distant part of him also wondered if Cade was telling him for a reason.

Elias lay a hand on the side of Cade's neck, holding him gently. "If we did do more stuff. If we liked the sexual stuff, why not? We're already compatible, and to be blunt, I have a love for you already. Why would I turn away the chance to find out if that love can grow into something else, and have someone to spend my life with who I know is my best friend?"

Cade stared up at him, wide-eyed. "Jesus, Elias."

"What, what'd I say?"

Cade cleared his throat. "Just, Jesus. That's, really fucking sweet."

"It's...the truth," Elias said, bewildered.

Cade smiled up at him. "I know. You don't lie unless you're doing it for my benefit, apparently."

Elias smiled back, glad to see the warmth back in Cade's face. "So, I hate to put it on you, but I'm following your lead. You know where I stand."

Cade took a deep breath, reaching out to lay a hand on Elias' chest. There was a momentary flash of strangeness to have so strong a hand against him, touching him so intimately. But he didn't care, Cade's warmth radiated through Elias' shirt, and the weirdness washed away.

It was Cade.

"We have time," Cade began. "Tonight. We can...figure things out."

"Figure them out?" Elias asked.

Cade stepped closer, a little hesitantly, but he did it. "You, me. Sex."

Elias' chest tightened. "You want to sleep with me?"

"I want to see what we like and what we don't. I want to find out if it's all or nothing. And right now, I'm not seeing any limits."

Elias' eyes widened. "You...you what?"

"Let's just say I've had a few eye-openers over the past few days. And maybe I'm being an idiot for holding back just because it seems weird at first. Kissing you is weird, but it's only weird because it *isn't* weird, you know?"

"I'm familiar with the feeling."

"But kissing you feels great, amazing. And when we...fooled around, I liked that too. Your hands on me, hearing you..."

And he was hard all over again.

Cade stared up at him, laying his other hand on Elias' chest. "We go with it tonight. We see where it goes. If either of us has to tap out because it's just plain weird, instead of weird because it's okay, then we say so, and we stop. Deal?"

Elias' heart thundered in his chest. "Okay. But now it's my turn."

"Your turn?"

Elias bent forward, gently grasping the back of Cade's head and pulling him forward. Once again, that electric pleasure shot through him, curling in his gut and becoming fire. He sucked in a breath as they carefully parted their lips. For a moment, their mouths fumbled as they tried to figure out how their tongues should work. Cade gave a soft laugh, and Elias took the opportunity to take over. He almost expected Cade to protest, but instead, he earned a soft sound from the other man and felt him press closer to him.

"Bossy," Cade murmured.

Elias chuckled. "I get the feeling you liked it."

"I'm not afraid to let someone take over if they want to," Cade muttered.

Elias glanced over his shoulder. "I think...we would do better on a bed for this."

"And just what kind of boy do you think I am?" Cade asked.

"The kind who's interested in his first gay experience with his best friend who's also having his first gay experience."

"That's fair."

Cade's tone was light, but Elias could still sense the wariness in him as they walked toward the bedroom. Despite Elias swearing up and down, he was ready for more, even he felt a fluttering in his gut. The kiss had gone a long way toward making him feel better about everything and very interested in seeing what else felt good between them. Yet his mind kept pacing over the feel of Cade's stubble against his cheek, the feel of muscle on Cade's chest. It was all so different, and yet, he was still hard.

Nervous or not, that was good enough for him.

Cade stood at the edge of the bed, staring down at it as Elias entered the room. Knowing it was better to keep their momentum going before either of them had second thoughts, Elias pressed against him from behind. Cade's back was hard, filled with muscle, but Elias only noticed briefly. Instead, he focused on the soft breath Cade released when Elias pressed his lips to the man's neck, sucking it gently.

Cade wriggled slightly. "I can...feel your dick."

"Well, it is hard," Elias mumbled against his neck.

"I know, it's…"

"Weird?"

Cade snorted, twisting his arm to reach behind him and grip onto the bulge at the front of Elias' pants. Elias' breath hissed out against Cade's neck, pleasure rippling through him gently as Cade's fingers explored. To his credit, Cade didn't pull away but instead turned around to face Elias and kiss him again. Elias pressed down into the kiss, holding Cade close to him.

"Not too weird," Cade admitted to him.

"Let's get these clothes off," Elias suggested.

"Rip the bandage off?" Cade asked.

"Something like that."

Elias had undressed in front of Cade more times than he could count. None of those times had been as nerve-wracking and yet erotic as this time. Elias peeled his shirt off, watching as Cade did the same and bent to pull his pants off. The muscles of Cade's back shifted beneath his pale skin, and Elias couldn't help but run a hand over Cade's flat stomach when he stood up. The faint hairs on his stomach brushed against Elias' palm, and he felt the stomach muscles twitch.

"Ticklish?" Elias asked softly.

"Not really, just…" Cade trailed off.

Remembering their promise, Elias held back from asking if Cade was okay. He trusted the man to tell him the truth. Instead, he kept his hand moving, slipping it down, past the band of Cade's underwear. Cade's cock was rock hard and pulsed against Elias' fingers as they wrapped around it.

"That feeling I remember," Cade breathed, leaning closer to Elias.

"So do I," Elias said, running a finger gently over the leaking head.

"Shit," Cade moaned.

Elias finished taking his clothes off, reluctantly pulling his hand away from Cade while he did so. He was finding that so long as he was hearing Cade, knowing the man was enjoying himself, the weirdness of the situation melted away quickly.

He also knew what he wanted to try next.

"Sit down," Elias said.

Cade did so, staring up at him. His eyes widened when Elias knelt before him, scooting closer, so he was between Cade's legs. Having never given a blowjob before, Elias wasn't entirely sure what he was doing. He'd had enough of them to take a good guess at it though.

Gripping the base of Cade's cock, Elias leaned forward. The tip was still leaking, a sure sign they were doing something right. Knowing he had to get it over with to find out, Elias ran his tongue over the leaking head, tasting him. He paused, cocking his head.

"What?" Cade asked.

Elias looked up, shrugging. "Not bad."

Cade looked down at his dick and laughed. "I hadn't even thought about that part."

Elias raised a brow. "You felt the need to specify that

you've had something up your ass before, but didn't consider what cum tasted like?"

Cade's eyes darted between his cock and Elias' face. "I'm a little focused on the fact that I'm really liking where you're headed with this. We can talk about butt stuff later."

Elias snorted, but he wasn't going to pass up continuing, not when it seemed like Cade was loosening up. Leaning forward once again, he wrapped his lips around the head of Cade's cock, tasting him once again. The low moan Cade gave was further encouragement to experiment with swirling his tongue around, and he wasn't surprised when Cade's noise deepened.

Apparently, witnessing and being on the receiving end of a blowjob was good enough to get started.

Emboldened, Elias leaned forward, feeling Cade's cock slide along his tongue and into his throat. After a few inches, he felt his throat tense, already prepared to spasm at the intrusion. That was fine, Elias had seen that happen more than once when he'd been receiving. Rather than push it, he backed away to suck on the head and bow forward again. Meanwhile, he used his hands in rhythm with his mouth, jerking Cade as he sucked and licked.

Once he'd built a good rhythm, he found the pattern that worked best. Cade hunched over him, hands gripping onto Elias' back and moaning fiercely. His cock throbbed against Elias' tongue. While the dick sucking itself wasn't all that thrilling to Elias', his cock jerked against his thigh every time Cade let out a deep moan.

"Okay, okay, you win," Cade gasped out, pushing at Elias' shoulders.

Elias pulled off quickly. "What? What'd I do?"

Cade eyed him. "You sure you've never done that before?"

"Uh, no. I can promise you that."

"Fast fucking learner, then."

Elias chuckled, pushing up to kiss Cade. "Well, bravo for me then. And for you."

"Apparently," Cade murmured against his mouth.

"And what was that about me winning?"

Cade looked down at Elias' crotch and then up at his face. "Uh, you got lube?"

Elias stared and then blinked when he realized what Cade was asking. "Oh. Yeah, and condoms."

Cade hesitated, and Elias quickly added, "Don't push it, Cade, I'm okay like this."

Cade shook his head. "No, no. I mean, that felt good as fuck. And I want to return the favor, but I kinda...well, if that felt good when you did it, and butt stuff with other people felt good, then I'm thinking it would with you. And I'd really just like to try while I've got the courage."

"Can we just call it anal, or fucking? Butt stuff is getting weird."

Cade snorted. "Anal then."

Elias bent forward, kissing Cade once more. "And I think that courage is called horniness."

"Whatever it is, it's got me ballsy enough to try. And I hesitated because...bare?"

Elias raised a brow. "No condom?"

"I'm clean," Cade told him softly.

Elias smiled, brushing Cade's face gently. "If you say you are, then you are. I trust you a hundred percent."

"Okay."

Elias nodded, not entirely sure if escalating was a good idea. As he retrieved the bottle of lube from the nearby drawer, he couldn't deny a thrill of excitement either. Cade in his mouth had been okay, but the sounds Cade had made were even better. And using the same logic that Cade had used, fucking someone felt good. So he could have both the pleasure of fucking and the added, increasingly addictive sound of Cade's enjoyment.

"Probably should uh, prep first," Cade said when Elias sat on the bed beside him.

"Okay, lay back."

Cade raised a brow. "Yeah?"

"I've done anal before, Cade," Elias told him.

Cade's eyes widened. "What? But I…"

Elias snorted. "I've given it. Nothing's been up my ass. But if you want to try it on me…"

Cade shook his head. "Nope, I volunteered. I've got the experience…and the big mouth."

"Just remember our deal," Elias told him as he opened the bottle.

"Just…do it."

"You sure know how to seduce a guy."

Cade scowled at him. "Don't fuck with me."

Elias pressed a lubed finger against Cade's hole. "Just fuck you?"

Before Cade could answer properly, Elias gently pressed a finger forward. Cade sucked in a sharp breath, and Elias froze.

"Cold," Cade told him with a stuttered laugh.

Elias nodded, pressing his finger forward more. He wasn't surprised that Cade didn't react much, one finger wasn't terrible, especially if Cade had the experience to know what to expect. Elias still took his time, easing the single digit in and out of the other man, gently opening him. When it came time for the second finger, Cade let out a soft noise. Elias didn't stop that time, drawing another low sound from Cade as the second finger slid in completely. Elias patiently waited, stuck between wanting to make it easy on Cade, and a little caught up in the heat of Cade's body. He moved his fingers, spreading them apart and sucking in a breath at the grip around him.

When his fingers brushed against something inside Cade, the man gave a slight jerk and a real moan. Elias knew enough about the body to know what he'd hit, and just to make sure, he brushed the same spot again. Cade's cock jumped, and fluid leaked from the tip as the man held tight to the mattress. He was able to distract Cade enough with that to add a third finger.

"And that's why I was okay with...anal play," Cade said with a shaky laugh.

"I've been missing out," Elias said.

"You got big fingers."

"Sorry."

Cade shook his head. "Don't get me wrong, I'm still working through that it's you. But you know, I'm okay with that."

"You sure?"

"I'm really digging the face you make when you're enjoying yourself and focused."

Elias looked up, looking at Cade's red face and smiling. "And you've kept me rock hard because of your noises. Weird?"

"Yeah, but we're not stopping."

"That mean..."

"Yeah, but uh…"

Elias gently pulled his fingers free, chuckling. "Me on my back?"

Cade nodded, and Elias did as he was told. Lying on his back, cock sticking straight up, he watched his friend. Cade took the bottle of lube and squirted some into his hand. His fingers shook, but his grip was firm as he wrapped it around Elias' cock. Elias sucked in a breath, unable to help the low moan as Cade's fingers glided over the length of his cock.

Damn, he didn't even care if this was outside their norm, Elias could get used to it.

Apparently satisfied with his work, Cade got up, straddling Elias' hips. Reaching below him, he took hold of Elias' cock and held it steady. Elias reached out, holding onto Cade's thighs and watched him. Sweat shone on Cade's forehead and chest, but the man's face was furrowed in a look of determination. He eased back, pressing Elias' cock against him. For a moment, there was nothing, and then Elias gave a soft gasp as the grip of Cade's ass wrapped around him.

"Oh shit," Elias groaned as another inch slid into Cade.

Cade let out a puff of air. "Wooh, okay, that's uh, definitely bigger than the toys."

Elias wanted to tell him to stop if that was the case, but Cade leaned back again, slipping more of Elias into him. Cade stopped and took another few breaths before continuing. Elias' fingers dug into Cade's thighs as the grip continued slowly working its way down his shaft, engulfing him. All Elias could do was hold tight and wait until he felt Cade settle into his lap, having taken him completely.

Cade leaned forward, pressing his hands against Elias' chest with a sigh. "Whew, that was...an experience."

Elias looked up at him. "Are you okay?"

"Believe it or not, yeah. Bigger than the toys, but that's...not a bad thing."

Elias grinned. "I'm a little impressed."

"Be impressed if I get through this."

With that, Cade inched his hips up, before letting himself fall down slowly. It was enough to shut Elias up, and his grip on Cade's thighs tightened once more. Cade continued, the tense look on his face melting away as he repeated the act. His arms began to shake, and his breath came out in short bursts as he raised himself even higher and let himself fall.

On the last, Cade raised up until Elias was nearly out of him completely before letting himself fall.

"Oh fuck," Cade gasped.

"Cade?" Elias asked, trying to keep himself still.

Cade shook his head. "We gotta roll. I can't do this. You gotta."

"Okay, just let me pull out, and we can try me."

Cade grunted. "No, I mean, you do the fucking. This...you...just, you do it."

Elias raised a brow, but he wasn't going to argue. As unsure as he had been about blowing Cade, he was confident about being able to fuck him. He took hold of Cade's hips and rolled them both, pressing Cade against the bed. The movement shifted his cock inside Cade, drawing a moan even more enticing than the last ones.

"Holy shit," Elias muttered.

"Go," Cade said, winding his legs around Elias' hips.

Elias did as he was told, pulling his cock out and then gently pushing himself back in. Cade's ass didn't grip him as fiercely as when Cade had first started, but it still held onto Elias tight. The heat and tightness had Elias' body demanding he move, demanding he do *something*. Slowly but surely, he began to work up a pace.

Below him, Cade's head pushed back against the bed, his hands tight around Elias' arms. Cade moaned, clenching his eyes shut as Elias buried himself again. Given confidence, Elias began to thrust in earnest, pulling back halfway and driving himself forward. The more he gave Cade, the louder Cade became.

Elias had never seen Cade in a moment of pleasure. He had never seen the man's forehead beaded with stress, deep moans falling from his lips, as he panted and encouraged as best he could. Cade's legs pulled hard against his waist as though trying to yank Elias in as he fucked him. Elias buried himself, building strength and confidence as Cade bucked and thrust against him.

Cade's eyes snapped open, and without warning, he yanked Elias down toward him. His back twinged from the sudden movement but was lost as Cade's mouth pressed hungrily against his. Cade's body went taut around him, bearing down on him fiercely and yanking a desperate moan from him. Below him, Cade's cock jerked, and the man cried out, cum spurting between them as Cade rocketed into an orgasm.

"Cade," Elias warned through gritted teeth.

"Do it," Cade moaned, still gripping Elias tight.

A few more thrusts, drawing whimpers from Cade, and Elias bowed over him with a cry. His body went wire tight as he came deep inside him. Elias called out Cade's name as his orgasm washed through him, wiping away all thought, save for the whispering of his name from Cade's lips.

When it was done, Elias sagged, carefully removing himself from Cade. Using his flagging strength, he grabbed a towel from his shower earlier and carefully wiped Cade and then himself. Tossing it aside, he knelt on the bed, still trying to catch his breath. Below him, Cade lay on his back, eyes clenched shut, and his chest heaving.

Elias reached out tentatively, laying a hand on Cade's waist. "Cade?"

Cade's eyes opened, searching until they found Elias' face. "Hey…"

"You okay?" Elias asked softly.

Cade grinned. "I'm...not completely sure what I am right now. I'm going to just go out on a limb and say I'm great."

"Really?" Elias asked, nervousness bleeding away.

Cade chuckled. "I can't...really move my legs, and it feels like someone blew my brains out. Or fucked them out rather.

That was...shit, that was not nearly as weird as I thought it would be."

Elias eased himself down onto the bed, lying beside Cade. "Agreed. I kind of forgot about the weirdness after a little bit."

Cade looked at him, face shining and hair soaked with sweat. "So, you're good?"

Elias leaned over, drawing Cade to him and kissing him. A smile twitched at the corner of his mouth as he felt Cade melt against him, giving in to the kiss easily. Elias pulled Cade even closer so he could wrap his arms around him and hold the man tight. Cade wasn't all that much smaller than him, but he fit so well against Elias' body.

Cade let out a soft noise. "Of course, you're a cuddler."

Elias held him tight, reveling in the sudden contentment washing through him. God, they could actually do this.

"Damn right I am," Elias said, closing his eyes.

"Good," Cade said simply.

Elias held him close, not letting him go even as his exhaustion started to take him over. He knew they still needed to talk, and probably figure a few things out, but that could wait until later. For the moment, he was happy to hold Cade close to him, feeling his breathing deepen, and to know that he was with someone who loved him.

CADE

*W*hen he woke, the room was dark save for the moonlight streaming through an open window. His head was buried against Elias' chest, with an arm wrapped around Cade to keep him in one place.

Cade lay there, smiling in the dark as he paid attention to all the places where their bodies touched. The arm on his back, their legs wrapped around one another, and even the deep breaths from Elias that ruffled Cade's hair. There was a noticeable dull ache coming from his ass too, but he didn't have to question that one.

As a matter of fact, the ache brought a broader smile to his face. By God, he'd set out to see what they could get up to, and they'd done just about everything. Of course, there was still the case of him having to try giving a blowjob, and even finding out if Elias could take Cade, but what did that matter? Cade had full-on made out with Elias, got a blowjob, and let the man fuck him, everything else was just details. Admittedly, they were details that had his once sleeping cock stir to life again, but details all the same.

He lay there in the dark, wrapped up in Elias' arms, and

realized he'd never felt more at peace. Who cared if he had just thrown away his sizable monthly allowance, and pretty much cut himself off from his family? Who cared if his sexuality was a mess at the moment, and he still couldn't tell if it was him being bi or just attracted to Elias. Cade was warm and wrapped around a person who loved him and who Cade loved dearly, that's all that mattered.

Well, and a pressing call to use the bathroom.

Cade gently pulled himself out from under Elias' arm. Untangling his legs required a bit more finesse, but he managed it without shaking Elias too much. Slipping off the edge of the bed, he padded his way to the bathroom. He didn't bother turning the light on as he entered, no need to blind himself when he already knew where the toilet was. Once done, he washed his hands, dried them, and made his way back into the bedroom.

When he eased down onto the bed, Elias' hand came out and took hold of his leg. "Hey."

Cade smiled. "Hey."

"You came back," Elias murmured.

Cade's chest squeezed. "Yeah, of course."

"Good."

Elias tugged on him, and Cade allowed himself to be pulled back toward Elias. The big man's arm wrapped around him again, drawing him close. This time Elias lay behind him, his front curled around Cade's back. Elias' warm body pressed against him, holding him tight as Elias buried his face in Cade's hair and sighed contentedly. It wasn't the first time someone had cuddled him from behind, but it was the first time he'd done it and had a guy's dick pressed against his ass.

Cade smirked, wrapping an arm around Elias and snuggling closer. It wasn't just any dick, it was Elias'. And while he wasn't sold on all dicks being wonderful, he was definitely sold on Elias' being great. It had done the job and then some only hours before, and hopefully, if Cade hadn't totally screwed everything up by waiting too long, there might be more, a whole lot more.

"Sleep," Elias murmured thickly.

And he did and found out later that waking up for the second time in a row in Elias' arms proved to be as wonderful as the first. Though that had come with Elias having already beaten him awake in the first place. The man was smirking down at him, running a hand over Cade's stomach until he'd woken up.

"What are you doing?" Cade asked.

"Touching you," Elias answered.

"I see that."

"You asked."

"Why?"

"Because I like touching you."

Cade bumped him with an elbow and grinned. "I'll take that as a good thing."

Elias' hand slid further down Cade's body, wrapping his fingers around Cade's cock. "A very good thing."

Cade's stomach flipped, and his cock hardened. "Oh, I see."

He wasn't one to argue with a bit of morning fun, but somehow, he hadn't pictured Elias as the frisky type. The man was barely a person when he first woke up. Yet for the first time, Elias looked well-rested, and his eyes were sparkling with desire.

For him.

Cade rolled onto his back, running a hand over Elias' broad chest. "Got something in mind, do you?"

Elias slipped down further, till his mouth hovered over Cade's cock. "Need to make sure we can do everything, right? Well, I didn't get to swallow last night."

Cade smirked. Probably because the man had come inside Cade instead. The thought barely touched on weird, not when Elias' mouth was so close to his cock.

Cade sucked in a breath. "I guess we should find out."

Turned out, swallowing wasn't a problem.

* * *

THE AFTERNOON SUN beat down on them on the terrace of the cafe. They'd chosen a table without an umbrella. Considering the growing heat, Cade was glad he'd chosen a frozen smoothie. Across from him, Elias was sipping slowly on some frozen coffee concoction that he'd rattled off with ease. Even the barista behind the counter had been impressed and a little taken aback, but not so much that she didn't give Elias' broad frame an appreciative second glance.

"Pretty sure that barista is trying to get you alone," Cade said, glancing into the cafe.

Elias raised a brow. "What?"

"The girl who took your drink. The one who drooled over you," Cade clarified.

Elias snorted. "She was not drooling."

"Right, she just couldn't keep her eyes off you once she caught sight of you," Cade said.

Elias watched him for a moment, a small smirk raising the corner of his mouth. "Is that...jealousy I'm hearing?"

Cade choked on his next sip, sputtering. "What? No!"

Elias took another drink. "I think you might be."

Cade felt his face get hot. "I am not. Just stating facts. I know checking out when I see it."

Elias set his cup down. "I guess this is going to be the best segue I'm going to find, but what about us?"

Cade blinked. "What?"

"Us Cade. You and me."

185

"I'm aware of what 'us' means."

Elias sighed. "Look, I know it's early to be talking like this. But I'm not going to lie, last night was…"

"Amazing," Cade finished for him.

Elias grinned. "Mind-blowing works too. I mean, I've had some great sex before, but that was…yeah, that was something else."

Cade chuckled, feeling his face warm again. It's not like he was going to argue with the man. Cade supposed it wasn't that much of a leap to go from enjoying a girl liking to bring a toy to the bedroom to having a guy fuck him. Then again, if it had been anyone else, Cade would have declined immediately. With Elias, however, it had definitely been a mind-blowing experience, and that included the literal blowjob that morning.

Elias leaned his elbows on the table. "But what I mean is, is that it? Do we just…fuck around, hang out, and that's it?"

Realization struck Cade. "Oh…you mean…"

Elias grimaced. "Yeah."

Cade couldn't help his light laugh. "I mean, if we were an actual item, would we really be doing anything different than that?"

Elias frowned. "It would feel different."

Cade knew what he meant, but he hadn't been able to hold back his amusement. In truth, he'd joked before that dating Elias would be the easiest thing ever if it wasn't for the fact that they were both straight. Now it seemed that they weren't quite as straight as they thought, or something along those lines. Cade still wasn't sure exactly what their sexuality was, but after the night before, he realized it was probably pointless trying to figure it out. They'd enjoyed themselves, and now Cade's mind was no longer obsessing over whether or not it was weird, and more on the shape of Elias' hand, and how he could get it around his waist again.

Cade set his cup down and gently took Elias' hand in his. "I know. You mean actually date. Be monogamous."

Elias frowned at their hands. "Now that you put it like that, I guess not much would change for us, would it? Just those few things."

"Well, and sharing a bed in a whole different way," Cade said, running his fingers over Elias' hand.

Elias grinned. "I liked it. Waking up with you beside me."

"So did I," Cade readily admitted.

Maybe he wasn't going to adjust to everything overnight. There were bound to be moments when he couldn't help but think how strange the whole thing was. But if he had to deal with a few disconcerting thoughts, and got to look forward to that same feeling when Elias had kissed him, or when he'd woken up beside the man, warm and safe, then he would take them.

"I want to keep going," Cade told him.

Elias' face brightened. "Yeah?"

"I want to keep finding out more stuff that works for us. I want to prove to my former, freaked out self that it was all stupid and pointless. I loved last night, and I loved this morning. Everything about it just felt so...*right*, you know? Being around you has always felt right, I really shouldn't be all that surprised that it led to this point," Cade told him, squeezing his hand.

"That was the best night's sleep I've had in weeks," Elias told him softly.

"And I've never felt better. Maybe that should tell us we're doing something right. So let's keep going, let's find out. If it leads us to being committed, so be it. But I want us to have the chance to find out without any expectations. Christine already knows the truth, so we don't have to be as paranoid or as dedicated to keeping up appearances," Cade said.

Elias straightened. "What?"

Cade snorted. "Sorry, I didn't have a chance to tell you. She and I talked the other day. She knows everything, and she's apparently really sorry that it caused so much trouble."

"And you believe her?"

"Weirdly enough, I do. She's the one who finally gave me the push to stop being so stupid and make the leap. Honestly, I probably owe her a gift for that one, because she was absolutely right."

Elias shook his head. "Hard to believe she was the one who helped."

Cade wrinkled his nose. "In a weird way, she was the one who started it all. If you think about it, her pulling that shit is what got us in this spot in the first place. Not that I'll thank her for that, but the advice? Yeah."

Elias shrugged, looking down at their entwined hands. "Well, maybe I will."

"Is that my name I hear over there?"

Christine's voice brought Cade upright and looking around. She was approaching from the street, a big smile on her face. Behind her came the stone-faced visage of his mother. Pamela glanced their way with a sharp gaze, landing on the table where Cade and Elias' hands were still clasped together. Cade kept his grip on Elias' hand, staring his mother in the face as the woman marched into the cafe without a word.

Christine sighed. "She really is unhappy."

"She can get the fuck over it," Elias grunted.

Cade blinked, having never heard Elias say anything negative about Pamela. "What he said."

Christine chuckled. "I have a feeling that's the last thing she'll do. She absolutely refuses to speak of you whatsoever. Apparently, you had words?"

Cade wrinkled his nose. "Quite a few, and none of them nice."

"Ah, well, that would certainly explain it. Certainly has made her more determined in her planning, though all her upcoming plans don't involve you," Christine noted.

"I think I'm out of the will," Cade said.

Christine tapped her chin. "And that's what you want?"

Cade looked her in the eye. "Christine. I hate your life, I hate the life she leads, and I hate the life you all wanted for me. If I have to be poor to have Elias and my life, then I'll be poor."

Elias wrinkled his nose. "Your income isn't that low."

Christine chuckled, reaching out to stroke a hair out of Cade's face. "Good for you Cade. A shame, but I can't begrudge you your happiness."

Cade smiled at that. "Thank you, Christine."

Christine turned, and her smile dimmed as she eyed Elias. "And you. Be good to him, or I'll absolutely ruin you."

Elias stared at her as she turned and marched off into the cafe. Once inside, she waved to them cheerily, much to the obvious irritation of his mother.

Elias grunted. "I think she's starting to grow on me."

Cade laughed. "Yeah, weird isn't it?"

Elias stood up, waiting for Cade before taking his hand again. For Cade, walking hand in hand with Elias in public was far easier than kissing Elias the night before had been. Yet it left him feeling as warm and content as waking up with the man wrapped around him had. That sense of rightness grew thicker with every passing moment they spent together since Cade had finally given in and thrown himself over the edge.

"Matt invited us along for a few drinks tonight," Elias said as they waited at the crosswalk.

"Us? You've already told him?" Cade asked.

Elias grinned. "No, the invitation was for me and you, but I don't think he meant it as a couple thing. Says he wants us to actually hang out with him and his boyfriend, and just...have fun."

"Hm, I smell a double date," Cade said.

"Might be, that a problem?"

The signal lit up for them to walk, and they stepped out onto the street, hand in hand.

Cade grinned. "If I'm with you, no."

ELIAS

One Year Later

He groaned as he threw himself in one of the mess hall's seats. The summer had been a hot one, and despite being a coastal city, things had dried out. There had been at least two wildfires and three home fires in the past week alone. Elias was desperately hoping for the end of shift to hit before the alarm bell went off again.

Matt slumped into a chair across from him, looking just as drained. "Is it bedtime yet?"

Elias chuckled, leaning forward onto his arms. "God, don't I wish?"

He would love nothing more than to stumble his way back home. Back to the apartment he'd once lived in for so long by himself, albeit with a frequent visitor. Now Cade lived with him and had been for pretty much the entire year. It had become official eight months ago, with Cade giving up the apartment he barely used, throwing out some of his crap, and moving the rest in. It was inevitable, and it was easier on Cade's finances since he was no longer receiving money from his parents. That was a fact Cade was happy to tell anyone when the subject came up.

Elias desperately looked forward to crawling into their bed and maybe convincing Cade to give him a good rub down.

"Cade chose a good day to have off," Matt said, sounding grumpy.

Elias snorted. "I made him do it. Dumbass has been working day in and day out, he needed a day off to just do something else."

"Well, tell him he's lucky to have someone like you to talk sense into him," Matt said, closing his eyes.

Davis stumbled in, grabbing a cup of coffee. "Sorry, but I'm here for another shift. Fuck I need this."

Elias waved him off. "Finish it, I'm going home."

"Oh, that explains why the boy toy is here," Davis said with a smirk.

Elias shook his head. "Why is it you don't call him by his name when he's not around?"

"Because it drives you nuts," Davis said, giving him a wink and strolling back out of the room.

"You know, as much as I like the fact that he's not being an ass anymore, I gotta say, I'm not sure I'm down with him poking me," Elias grumped.

"At least he's not Keith," Matt pointed out.

"Yeah, well, so long as Keith remembers what I told him last year, that's all I care about," Elias growled.

A warm pair of hands fell on his shoulders, followed by Cade's amused voice near his ear. "Have I ever told you how much I love it when you get grumpy?"

Elias looked up into Cade's sparkling hazel eyes. "And why's that?"

Cade looked over at Matt. "I'm sorry, Eli, I can't. There are children in the room."

Matt snorted, pushing out of his seat. "Oh, please, Cade. I was getting dicked down long before you ever thought about putting Elias in your mouth."

Cade stared at Matt as the man wandered out of the room. "Jesus. That's the kind of shit I'd expect *me* to say."

Elias snorted. "I think he's pretty tired."

"Apparently."

"What are you doing here, anyway? You're supposed to have the day off."

"Well, after a long lunch with Christine, I decided to head over here and take you back home."

Elias raised a brow. "I drove myself, remember?"

"And I took a cab. Which means I can drive you back, and you can relax. I heard about the fire over on Williams."

Elias sighed. "God. This has been a week. How was lunch?"

"It was good. Christine is asking about wedding planning, though."

"Uh, what?"

Cade laughed. "Don't worry, I told her that wasn't something we'd talked about. We're still at the boyfriend stage, not fiancés."

Elias grunted, smiling a little at the image of Cade standing at the altar in a tux. The image faded away as Cade bent over, kissing him soundly. Cade made to pull away, but Elias reached up, cupping the back of his head and deepening the kiss. Cade groaned against him, his fingers curling on Elias' neck.

"Hi," Elias whispered.

"Hey," Cade said.

"I'd really like to go home."

"I bet."

"Have some good food."

"I can whip us up something good."

"Fuck my incredibly hot boyfriend into the mattress."

Cade's pupils widened, and he grinned. "Easily given."

"And sleep until tomorrow."

Cade stepped back, holding out his hand. "Then come on."

Elias took his offered hand and stood up. "Or maybe a hot shower first."

"Feed you, then a nice bath with me in that big ass tub you had to have?" Cade asked.

"Oh, god, yes."

"I love it when you moan."

Elias wrapped an arm around Cade's waist. "And I just plain love you."

Cade leaned him into him as they walked out into the afternoon sun. "And I love you."